T0110313

THE
BLANKET
OF ICE

THE BLANKET OF ICE

GOLDIE & SHEETAL DUGGAL

PARTRIDGE

A Penguin Random House Company

Copyright © 2014 by Goldie & Sheetal Duggal.

ISBN: Hardcover   978-1-4828-1532-0
      Softcover   978-1-4828-1533-7
      Ebook   978-1-4828-1531-3

All rights reserved. No part of this book may be used or reproduced by any means, graphic, electronic, or mechanical, including photocopying, recording, taping or by any information storage retrieval system without the written permission of the publisher except in the case of brief quotations embodied in critical articles and reviews.

Because of the dynamic nature of the Internet, any web addresses or links contained in this book may have changed since publication and may no longer be valid. The views expressed in this work are solely those of the author and do not necessarily reflect the views of the publisher, and the publisher hereby disclaims any responsibility for them.

To order additional copies of this book, contact
Partridge India
000 800 10062 62
www.partridgepublishing.com/india
orders.india@partridgepublishing.com

CONTENTS

This book is dedicated to the memory of my father to whom I shall remain indebted.

Goldie Duggal

For my parents, who have always been an inspiration.

Sheetal Duggal

ACKNOWLEDGMENT

The catalyst that allowed us to complete this work was 'Francesco Pagot'.

Our sincere thanks go to Franz who motivated us to explore the idea of 'The Blanket of Ice'.

Without your encouragement and guidance this project would not have materialized.

Thank you for sharing your expertise and valuable advice.

We are grateful for your constant support and help.

"No one saves us but ourselves. No one can and no one may. We ourselves must walk the path."

Gautam Buddha

I

Divine Blessings

*A*mid the mountainous Zanskar Range, a remote valley in the eastern half of Jammu and Kashmir separates Zanskar from Ladakh.

This fabled land of White Copper, a place of extreme cold, snow leopards, spirits and monks, was, in winter, cut off from everything. Our hut, of mud and stone, insulated by dried grass and sticks, nestled into the glaciers.

Even the silence was cold, for all sound froze on these dark walls, reluctant to bounce in the air, afraid to fall to the ground like glass shattered by freezing wind.

The Room congested with a stove, clothes, blankets, vessels, buckets, some containers and wood; all in one room. The cracked walls depicted the story of survival through faded hues, bravely balancing the wooden logs on shoulders; yet standing still, embracing us in arms over the years.

Our four yaks Diki, Pema, Rinzin and Tashi covered with jute sacks, tethered in a corner of the room, piled up bundles of black, brown and grey fur. In incoherent darkness to distinguish between fur and jute was difficult.

I, with my sister Chime, mother Zampa and Father Norbu enveloped under the thickly woven grey and brown blanket; the warmness of blanket always tempted me to snuggle in the bed for longer.

Pampering, soft blanket touch is yet unforgettable; every knit of it spoke about the efforts Maa had taken once to weave the blanket of love.

We huddled together to keep ourselves warm in that freezing atmosphere. Father had wrapped me under his arm; Chime at his other side; camouflaged between Father and Maa; more warmed, more protected, her face buried under Maa's palm.

As a child, I always envied Chime for gaining more love and protection from Maa and Father.

Electricity was far beyond reach in our territory. Lit stove always kept the room warm; the heat coming from the yaks' dry dung burnt steadily, breathed out earthy smoke; burning my eyes.

In that smoke-filled blur room I could see Maa. It seemed she couldn't sleep well the other night; her deepened eyes spoke of her worries, the time had come; her grip around Chime was more tighten.

The enchanting noise of the gong piercing the smoky room resonated on the mud walls; disturbing my thoughts, awakening my spirit, from the nearest monastery. One of the Buddhist monks in his maroon robe had performed the first ritual of many, indicating the beginning of a new day.

'The gong quiets the devils and awakes humans', they say.

The *Stongdey's* gong was known for bass-like echoes and bone-shaking shudder. Just the sound of its immortal echo made the monastery remarkably sacred.

A pearly grey dawn and my Father awoke with the first stroke of the metallic gong, followed by his routine. I never witnessed a day when Father ignored the gong; maybe his responsibilities never allowed him to. I am unsure about my Father's age, could be forty or more. For us, his age was like the mountain, eternal and omnipresent.

Though his lined face betrayed hard life of labor, he was not old enough to stop working.

Through the years he never gave up and worked hard to fulfill our needs. Hard work especially of physical nature was the source of survival for almost all individuals here.

Struggling against harsh nature, the wind and the ice was our life in Zanskar.

Lazing on the bed with heavy eyes I was noticing my Father's fragile figure moving hurriedly with the first stroke of the gong. In his traditional maroon *'goncha'*, a costume that takes the form of a calf-length smock made of yak wool tied around a waist with a *'cummerbund'*—a traditional belt. He untied Tashi, Pema, Rinzin and Diki and escorted them out on to the verandah one by one.

Diki as usual tried to hold ground; the most pampered creature of all. Father took his time to pander Diki, scratching her nose slowly with his long, bony fingers, and then running fingers through her soft grey hairs.

"Lousy creature" I thought. With this extra pampering Diki finally decided to walk out of the room. Father followed her out.

Through the gap of the cracked wooden door of the room I could see Father pouring buckets of water into the wooden drums to feed yaks. Pema cleaned her hooves and opened grain cans before Father could open it. Father started milking them one by one to extract the precious liquid that we so readily craved each morning.

It was still dark and chilled. In the dim light of the stove, which was burning since last night, I noticed my Maa. A lady in her thirties, face like the soft glow of a lamp, eyes swollen with previous night's disturbing thoughts, awaken with no time to waste. She pulled up the blanket carefully on Chime and me.

Maa moved carefully, feeding yaks' dung into our dying, burning, still grunting stove. Flames licked and consumed yak discharge, devouring them like a hungry devil, of the kind inhabiting our crevasses and peaks.

Maa broke the dung with her bare hands, snapping the hard stuff easily and without effort. Flames flashed illuminating mother's face reflecting the worries she had buried deep inside her. The room again filled with the smoke making it warmer, which tempted me to sleep for more time. Picking up a wok like container which was placed on the wooden plank; our so called shelf in the kitchen that displayed metal plates, glasses, woks, Maa walked out of the room to collect the ice.

Back of my mind I knew Maa would come to wake me up. The thought was really disappointing.

Carrying the container in both of her hands Maa placed it near the stove. Rocks of ice plummeted into the container as Maa filled the copper pot to melt the cold diamonds, to make hot tea for us. The enormous receptacle on top of the dung-fuelled stove hissed as the ice started melting into water. She came to me first as I had thought.

"Wake up Kaba, wake up," Maa said.

It was so cold that my eyes struggled to open, glued together as if to protect the moisture inside.

Maa shook me again; "Kaba wake up or else I will put ice in your blanket now." She tried to shout in her soft voice. It was hard to get out of the bed during those chilly days for a boy of my age.

I was just ten. The conditions were winterish, which demanded my body stay in bed much longer. I sat in my bed staring at Chime. She tossed in the bed facing me; Chime, five years my junior, my sweet little sister was still snuggling inside her blanket. Her pink chubby chicks sunk in the soft grey furry cover, leisurely taking her time to get up. Her cherry like face was smiling even in her sound sleep.

She might have encountered her favorite dream; dream of wearing a brand new school uniform and going to school.

"She will again make me listen to her dream today. Such a chatterbox she is" my subconscious reared his mind.

Her mouth was half open like a letter 'O'. She never stopped talking, even when she slept.

It seemed, in considering her age Maa had granted her a few extra minutes to sleep. Cursing myself for being born as the eldest to Chime I got up, feeling drowsy as I walked toward the verandah to rouse myself.

Maa awakened Chime and led her to the verandah. Having filled the bucket of warm water she then sprinkled water on Chime's face; her pink cheeks turned into scarlet with the touch of hot water. I was still deciding whether to take a wash, fiddling with mug when suddenly Maa splashed water on my face. No doubt it shook my thoughts.

Irritated I faced her saying, "Maa, I am grown up enough now to wash my own face." Cupping my hands I splashed water on my face.

After supplying the yaks with fodder, Father brought milk-filled buckets carefully inside the room without splashing a single drop of it. Father's skill of handling those milk filled heavy buckets swiftly always amazed me.

Chime rushed over to the yaks to feed them again; it was her daily exercise. Pampering them she said, "I am going to Ladakh School this year with Kaba, Father is taking both of us. He has promised to buy me a school uniform. Do you know how far Ladakh is?" Raising toward Rinzin she murmured, "We have to walk many days on *'Chadar'* to reach the school."

Father was watching his innocent, bubbly daughter from the edge of the room. He knew her excitement to go to the school. His face darkened with the thought of sending his dearest Chime away from him for ten months. Father always had understood the importance of education and therefore decided to send both of us to Ladakh School, as there was no major school in entire Zanskar region despite of few monasteries.

I always loved Chime beside all my fights with her that occurs between any brother and sister. The thought that Chime would be accompanying me to Ladakh School delighted me the most.

"It is my fifth year of walking the *Chadar*, but this year it would be fun with Chime joining us; her continuous talks will keep us busy throughout our tiresome journey" I thought.

Maa sat near the burning stove; her deep brown eyes gazed at the metal teapot. Water was boiling in the pot, so as Maa's thoughts.

As the water boiled Maa added dry tea leaves into it and let it steep for a couple of minutes. She then added a heaping quarter of a teaspoon of salt and allowed it to simmer. Straining the tea grounds she poured the tea mixture into the turquoise green, stone studded kettle. Adding a spoonful of butter, covering it with silver lid she shook it for a while and served us 'Po cha'—our tea, in the deep blue, silver rimmed cups chased with delicate floral motif all over. I remember Maa using them only on the special occasions or on arriving guests. May be that was her way of giving us *send-off*, one of the important days in her life. Finding *Po cha* in the precious cup delighted Chime; she always was fond of the painted flowers. She giggled all the time while having tea. Mother was looking at Chime thoughtfully.

Winter's pale sunrise had given the mountains a pink tinted appearance . . .

We charged ourselves with seeking the Old Lady's blessings for our successful journey. Religiously every year we would go with Father to meet the oldest woman of the village; she was Haji. It was my fifth visit at her place.

We united in our beliefs.

Our world, in the valley was always shared with Gods and Demons; measures were protected so any changes would not provoke them. Therefore, we always consulted Haji before venturing on to *Chadar*. Everyone in the Zanskar valley believed Haji possessed a supernatural power. She could foresee eventualities.

We started walking, scanning the little stack of rocks that marked the route. Holding Father's right-hand Chime was trying to match up with his speed, failing to cope with it. I was following them with Maa.

Snow clung in the peaks above. And ahead, white parted, the cairns swirled the clouds climbing higher and higher, in and out. Horizon went for a moment and spun back. Step after step, the way slowly revealed itself, the top of the pass appeared. Yellow, green, red, white and blue prayer flags rose on bamboo wands, crackled in the wind; enlightening our mind, reflecting *'Panchmahabhutas'*; the five elements of nature: earth, water, fire, air and space that manifest our physical world, say monks.

We walked through the village for a kilometer or so and reached Haji's hut. Faded through time, only a hint of its former cobalt blue paint remained.

Sunrise filled the valley with a watery glow.

Thoughts started pouring through my mind, "What Haji would predict? Would she allow us to cross *Chadar*?"

"What if Haji wouldn't allow us to walk on the *Chadar*?" The depressing, unwelcome thought popped unbidden into my head.

Before entering the hut, Father told Chime, "My Dear, if you wish to go to school, keep quiet inside. Haji is going to pray for our safe journey. If you talk, her prayers will be interrupted and she will not allow you to go to Ladakh." Chime nodded with approval. Father knocked on the rustic wooden door twice, patiently.

Nervously holding Chime beside me, I was waiting outside Haji's hut, for fate to open its door for Chime's bright future. After a while it was opened. Haji was not surprised to see us, it seemed we were expected.

She broke into a warm smile of welcome.

A light blue and warm brown colored, faded rug was already laid out. We settled ourselves onto the floor on the rug. Chime in between Maa and Father, I on the other side of Maa. The rug was of a small size and knotted a woolen warp. The patterns were derived from Chinese prototypes consisting one or three circles on a central field, with a key pattern. The little tea—table *'Chogtse'* was in front of us painted gaily with bunch of flowers.

There was no unnecessary arrangement in the room. Rows of gleaming brass and copper pots aligned against dark walls.

The sandalwood aroma of lit incense sticks erased any negative energy around. A skylight through the ceiling allowed the morning sun to pour into the small, dark hall, creating a dramatic play on the old walls and across our laps.

Haji moved slowly to one corner; and retrieved four wooden glasses of water for us.

By the time we finished drinking, she had her mat unfurled in front of us. With its height reaching the brim, with her skinny fingers, narrowing her squinty eyes she made a thin wick out of dry, odorless wood and placed it into a metal lamp, heaped barley on it and carefully poured clarified, melted butter over it.

Father, clearing his throat said, "Haji, I am taking children to the school. This time Chime, too, is joining us."

Silence filled the room. Haji sat on the mat facing the lamp. Praying to the deities Haji recited, *"Om Ah Hum Vajra Guru Dhe Vadakki Nihum" Od' OdLi Sarva Ah Lo Ke Praha Dhe Naye Svan Bah"* several times, calling for answers . . .

A serene face under the thin veil of dry, wrinkled skin, lost in some other world. Over the years I saw her face growing more and more wrinkled.

Nevertheless, her enduring aura of reverence always filled the room.

Unable to understand the meaning of the mantra, I engaged myself scanning the hut. Behind Haji, through the wooden window frames I was watching grandly looming Himalaya's various *'Avatars'* . . . sometimes blue, sometimes grey, sometimes hiding behind cloudy curtains mysteriously.

Haji's mantra echoed in the room.

After almost twenty minutes, she opened her eyes, lighting the butter lamp, she remarked the shape of the flame. The lamp's yellow light turned dim, the flame guttered unsteadily and then separated in two. Without blinking an eye, Haji watched the flame; it first turned red, and then smothered itself.

Haji uttered, "Chime is a small girl. I feel it's too early to send her to school now. I don't feel good about sending such a young girl so soon."

Father was listening to her attentively. Hearing to Haji's answer Maa shifted her glance from Haji to Father.

Chime's face faded into pale pink after hearing Haji's verdict. She squirmed uncomfortably.

Father looked at Chime while replying to Haji, "Chime is five years old. Education is important too. Kaba was the same age when he went to school."

He paused and then continued, "Children in Ladakh start their education at the age of three to four. We are still behind." His voice was firm.

Before Father could finish his sentence, I interrupted, "Haji, I will be there in Ladakh School and will take care of Chime."

Haji looked at Chime and softly asked her, "Are you ready to walk on *Chadar*?"

Chime immediately replied jumping in her sit, "Yes. I am! I am excited to go to school. Please Haji, allow me to go . . ." She gulped the words the moment Father stared at her.

While praying to the deities, Haji said, "May God gives you the strength. You are grown up now Kaba, so take care of Chime. I pray for your safe journey. God bless you."

Chime's eyes widen with joy. Haji lit some fire with coal in a metal bowl, adding dry juniper branches, lighting the scented sticks. The room filled with sandalwood aroma and earthy coal smell. She read some mantras for us.

We touched Haji's feet and offered our prayers . . . with her blessings we dismissed.

We walked through the white powdered lanes, Chime's hand entangled in mine.

We spied all the houses in the village dressed in bright blue, yellow and red hues, adorned with edelweiss garlands . . . readying themselves for a famous Buddhists' *'Karsha-Gustor'* festival.

Under the glowing sky in the compound, women rehearsed their dance steps. Chime was speaking to everyone on the way: the valleys, the pebbled land, the painted houses, even telling the snow-capped trees that she was going to Ladakh School.

Chime was floating on air.

Her excitement poured into the valleys of Zanskar; the sun reflected in her eyes.

2

KARSHA-GUSTOR

One by one, Maa gathered our belongings into sacks, packed the extra pairs of socks she had woven for us. And then she washed a few vessels to pack food.

I folded my new school uniform carefully and packed inside the sack; my second uniform throughout five years schooling. I had eagerly waited for this new uniform.

I collected all my stationery and new books. Picking up a pen from my stationery box I started scribbling my name on all textbooks and notebooks admiring my own handwriting, feeling proud.

Yoko, my childhood friend arrived. In maroon *goncha*, his lean timid figure leaned against the door panel, hands folded behind, and his brown woolen monkey cap tilted to his right side.

His parents couldn't afford to send him to school; all he had to do was helping his father in barley fields and feed the only yak they had.

Sluggishly, he walked towards me. "What are you doing Kaba?" he asked.

"I am packing my bag for my journey to school," I replied.

He started packing my bag with me. While packing my clothes, Yoko observed the long blue, textured piece of cloth and asked, "What it is?"

I took the thing in my hands and said, "This is called a tie and people wear it like this . . ." I started showing him how to knot the tie. "Wait, I will show you my school picture where all the students are wearing it," I said.

Keeping the tie aside I started looking for the picture in my messy room. I looked all around the room; on the shelves, inside small wooden cupboard filled with clothes; I flipped through my old books but couldn't find it.

Yoko was busy trying the tie around his neck.

I called for my mother, "Maa, did you see my school picture anywhere?"

"School picture?" Maa questioned while washing vessels on verandah.

"Yes Maa, my school group picture. I am wearing school uniform in it. I can't find it," I uttered.

"Oh, school picture! Why do you need it now? I have kept it safely in a trunk," entering with vessels Maa said.

She kept the washed vessels on the kitchen shelf and hastily went over to an old aluminum trunk; Itched with blue floral motifs that the trunk contained dried pulses. The photo enveloped in an old notebook was sunk in deep; this was the safest place in our house!!

Maa picked it up; dusting it with her scarf she handed over the photo to me.

Suddenly, we heard Yoko yelling. I looked at him, he had fastened the tie around his neck far too tightly and was choking, holding tie with both of his hands; instead loosening it up he was tightening it hard. His face was red like an apple; his cap covering half of his face, mouth was left open.

I dropped the photo. Maa and I ran to him before he choked himself to death and I somehow untied it. The moment Yoko got rid of the tie he started panting. Maa hurried towards the kitchen like area and came with a glass of water. He drank it like he would never ever get water to drink.

That day I realized how important knowledge is. Any step taken without knowledge can turn into danger. After this incident I showed the school photo to Yoko but he was no longer interested in seeing it.

Chime, as usual, was talking to the Yaks outside; sharing her feelings with them.

"At last, Haji has granted me permission and I am going to school, isn't it wonderful?"

She said to Tashi who agreed with her, swaying her head from side to side. Turning towards Diki, who was busy munching on fodder, Chime continued, "Do you know the way to Ladakh School? We have to walk for many days on ice tracks to reach school. I won't be able to see you until next year." Suddenly her tone softened.

With sincerity, she told her favorites, Rinzin and Pema, "When I return home next year from Ladakh I will bring a neck chain for all of you. Be good and don't fight. Don't go too far and don't bother Maa. I am going to miss you."

First time since her childhood she was going away from them. They were her best friends.

14

Father called, "Kaba, come and help me pack the cheese." I dashed towards our cheese warehouse.

Our warehouse was a flat roof shaded place with muddy walls where we used to churn butter, amass cheese and then store it. On the roof, Father had stacked animal fodder-alfalfa and hay, together with the leaves of the wild iris in neat bundles.

Sunlight was peeping through the gaps of the wooden log ceiling; the only light source storeroom had. There was only one screen window; to avoid too much air movement which could draw moisture from cheese causing the surface crack and cheese to dry out, Father sometimes opened the window. A roughly fashioned wooden ladder remained permanently fixed in one corner. Large jute bins full of barley lined the far wall. Malty odor of barley mingled with heavy, pungent smell of butter and cheese.

In that dark room, standing against the wooden rack, Father was admiring the cheese blocks he had stored on the wooden shelves, wrapped in a cotton cloth. He carefully picked up one block, unwrapped and smelt it. "Delicious! This year I will surely get extra rice." He was talking to himself aloud.

My footsteps shook his thoughts. Turning at me he said, "Kaba, come here. Taste this season's cheese!" His eyes reflected his inner joy.

He then reached to the knife placed on the shelf and cut off a small triangular piece out of the circular cheese block. Placing it on my palm he said, "Eat . . . and tell me how it is!" I stuffed that entire piece into my mouth. Holding the cheese block Father was looking at me, his mouth half open with anticipation.

"Yumm . . ." closing the eyes, feeling the smooth, salty, gooey taste, I uttered. No doubt it was the best cheese I had ever tasted. All his love and attention had rewarded with delicious cheese.

"I will get rice, spices and wheat from market in exchange of this cheese. And I will pay off your school fees." He said.

"And of course Chime's school uniform and books for Chime," he further continued.

"Father, we will also get Maa a scarf this time." I said joyously.

"Sure, my son," he nodded.

Father was sure his over the years earned goodwill in the market would remain intact. Cheese contained unique flavor and a high fat like every year.

"My vendors will be pleased; I hope the demand for our cheese would increase this year," piling up cheese blocks Father said.

Every year he came to pick me up from school during winter vacation. He took the orders for cheese and butter from the vendors and supplied them two months later when he returned to drop me back to the school. During his last trip when he had come to pick me up, several vendors had given him an advance so he had to make sure to deliver the cheese on time this year. We were already running late by a week.

"Vendors would be waiting for cheese. We must reach soon to Ladakh," he said worriedly.

There was no way to communicate with vendors than starting our journey.

Placing two wooden containers on he asked me to clean them. Once I cleaned them he then laid a wet cotton cloth to add more needed moisture. Attentively, one by one, I picked cheese blocks from the shelf and handed over to Father. Father cautiously started placing them in containers, counting his efforts. The last block left which Father had cut for tasting. Handing over it to me he said contently, "Kaba, give this to your mother. Tell her it's her share." He then covered the containers with lid.

After prolonged ageing our cheese was read . . . it had taken him ten months to amass it all. Father closed warehouse door; left the cheese to loom in the darkness for one more day.

The sun had set in a blanket of purple velvet tones.

We needed to attend a festival at night before leaving for Ladakh.

Chime was still hanging around yaks on verandah. We entered the room. Maa was getting ready for the festival; she wore a full pleated woolen skirt.

"Maa, this is your share!" handing over the cheese block to mother I said. Quickly, Maa packed it in one wooden tin.

She then moved swiftly towards a wooden cupboard and removed our folded *gonchas* hidden underneath woolen rugs.

"Dress up Kaba, we are running late for festival." giving them to me she said.

I kept aside Father's *goncha* and unfolded mine; it was quite heavy.

Father freshened up and wore his well-preserved maroon, woolen *goncha*. A silver glimmer of piping at the boarder and collar distinguished it from his regular *goncha*.

I wore my *goncha*, slightly brighter red than Father's *goncha*. I was struggling hard to fasten the right side shoulder buttons of my own *goncha*.

Watching me struggling with buttoning, Father walked up to me; fastening my buttons he said, "Kaba, you are no more child, learn to fasten it." I shrugged.

My *goncha* was loose; I looked into the mirror that had a crack at the left bottom but was mounted on the frame studded with semi precious stone. I was trying to give a finishing look to my *goncha* with *cummerbund*—a traditional waist belt. Father had got it stitched in a bigger size so I could use it for at least coming two years. The crack effect of the mirror was running across my shoulder. My height allowed me to see myself till my chest. Jumping twice or thrice I attempted to have glance at my entire costume; all in vain.

Chime laughed at me. She always needed some reason to laugh at me. I frowned and ran behind to catch her. But as usual she managed to hide behind Father.

Maa yelled, "Kaba, hurry up. Yoko must be waiting for us."

Maa complimented her pleated skirt with a colorful *'bok'*-a shawl. She also wore a *'Perak'*, traditional headgear made of black lambskin; covered with a layer of thinner red felt all stitched together, covering the head like a cobra's hood. She had studded it with turquoise stones, arranging them closely in seven rows, the single biggest and best stone placed at the front point. The black ears at the sides intensified the impression. She completed her dressing by wearing semi-precious antique coral beads necklace with delicate flat earrings with tiny jingles hung from chains. She was looking groomed and elegant.

Looking at mother's attractive headdress, Chime demanded, delightedly, "Maa, I want to wear the headgear too. It's looking so beautiful. Where is my headgear?"

Maa soothed her by saying, "My dear, your grandmother had given it to me when I married to your Father. It is valuable possession and I will give you once you complete school."

Maa then dressed up Chime in a pleated skirt with yellow, blue flowers she had embroidered with thread. Admiring the yellow flowers on the skirt Chime questioned, "Maa, when would you teach me to do these flowers?" Yellow was her favorite color.

"Once you return from school. Now keep quiet and let me do your hair. We are running late," Maa said. Maa braided her hair into two long pigtails and tied them with yellow ribbons. Chime was looking like a bloomed flower in the valley.

To keep Chime away from an evil spirit mother gave her one bracelet and coral necklace as a strong amulet.

"Decoration is the best protection from evil forces" Maa used to say.

"Hurry up children; I don't want to miss prayers," Father said.

We then put on our 'Papu'—shoes made with yak hair, gaily decorated with the sole of yak leather. I wore my hat, eventually it was Father's hat, and he used to wear it when he was of my age.

All the way, I tried to balance my hat; it kept tilting towards the right corner. I knew, I had committed a mistake wearing it, but I had to flaunt something in the festival.

We stopped at Yoko's house on our way to the festival. Yoko dressed in his *goncha* like mine was waiting on the verandah with his father Lobsang.

Uncle Lobsang was quite tall and thin man. He lived in his own little world keeping his distance from everyone. He spoke only if required. I had hardly seen him smiling; it seemed he was weighing world on his shoulder. Seeing us waiting, Nyima aunty, Yoko's mother came out of the room balancing her headdress; it was looking heavy on her fragile figure; she was impeccably attired.

Nyima aunty and my mother were thick friends. She was kind, gentlewoman. Uncle Lobsang was a bit strict man, but not so strict to hate. Nyima aunty always spoke less in the presence of uncle Lobsang. Yoko possessed a face of his mother and nature of his father.

Uncle Lobsang and Nyima aunty were part of our family. Since my birth they had been around.

Entwining hands Yoko and I started walking through the pebbled lanes towards the monastery. Yoko kept looking at my hat through out the way.

"Why he is staring at my hat? Because I cannot balance it or he doesn't have any?" asked my mind. To avert his attention pointing out at one old woman I said, "Yoko, look at that old woman; she has worn so many stones on her *Perak*." As usual, Yoko's reaction was as cold as ice.

We started noting the costumes of the people while walking. Some were wearing coat of yaks' fur complementing their *goncha*. Older women had tied goatskin around their neck. Maa was talking her heart out to Nyima aunty, following Father who was walking with Chime; talking as always; answering Chime's queries. Uncle Lobsang reached far ahead; his lean body racing up with wind.

Distance shortened; descending from the ridges we reached the *'Karsha'* monastery that hugged a steep mountainside. We climbed the long steep steps of *'gompha'*—a meditation room. Walking through *'stupas'*—a dome—shaped Buddhist Shrine, which were sitting aside the path we came across eight to twelve feet high, five to six feet diameter prayer wheels etched with sacred mantras. People were spinning them as they walked clockwise around to develop compassion and wisdom.

Chime, Yoko and I ran towards the praying wheels to spin them. But they were too heavy to rotate; Father helped us to spin. Together we recited the most intense and valuable mantra: *'Om Mani Padme Hum.'*

Mantra harmonized the environment; the blessings of mantra invoked our spirits.

Colorful paintings enriched the shrines.

The entire Zanskar valley had gathered. All men wore maroon colored woolen *gonchas* with hats and women wore pleated woolen skirt like gowns with shawls or scarves, *Perak* and antique jewelry. Likeness in costumes of all men and women reflected the unity and equality among the same vicinity.

Walking through the balcony painted an unusual shade of blue, we lounged ourselves on the steps of the prayer room in front of a heavy wooden door. The room was beautiful, clean and carpeted. The Lamas unfolded a painting intricately embroidered in gold and colorful threads on an orange cloth depicting Buddha surrounded by his tutelary deities.

The temple door stood open and at the distant end of the prayer room gleamed the altar, gilded with dozens of lit yak-butter lamps.

Few Lamas were moving up and down serving salt tea with heavy copper kettle, before one of them could reach us tea got over; he again ran down to fill the kettle.

Two young monks then blew the *'dung-chen'*—the long Tibetan horns through cupped hands, trumpets blasted joined by deep gongs. Conch shell horns moaned echoes over the valley. On the opposite wall older monks sitting in a row with drums and cymbals were creating the profound and discordant sounds. Lamas wearing red and yellow robes and brocade hats sat in lines started chanting the evening prayers.

Chime and I were giggling, pointing out at shaven-headed boys; Yoko sat calmly, preparing himself for prayer. Father asked me to keep quiet and concentrate on prayers.

The prayer chanted in the temple sounded in minds: *"Om Mani Padme Hum."* We fell down our face, prostrated, and then we stood, hands over the head, palms then coming together across the chest again falling to the floor. We rose and fell, before the altar.

One step after the other in slow synchrony with the drums *dum, dum, dum, dum* . . . . Conch sounded again *aroonh, aroonh, aroonh; bong, bong, bong* followed the gong . . . all-climaxing in clashing cymbals.

All six Lotus petals centered a lesson. *'Om'*—the call for generosity, a giving that we must make to overcome our pride. The monks called it to remember the values, control our desires.

Around the prayer flag and fire, middle of the courtyard, slow but periodically frenetic dances began to the rhythm of the music.

Father met his old friend, uncle Yonten who had come from *'Lingshed'* village with his wife and two daughters. Father was happy to see him after a year.

He told him, "I am going to drop Chime to Ladakh School this year. We are leaving tomorrow. You should send your daughters to school. Whenever I see Kaba in school uniform I feel proud, he looks a gentleman." Uncle Yonten nodded with approval looking at me; smiling.

"Norbu, I will try next year to send my daughters to school. I am happy for you; you are taking such an important step in life. Next year, when we meet here, you tell me about how it goes with Chime in school. We will go together to Ladakh to drop them," he uttered. Father patted him and both embraced each other.

Colorfully dressed Lamas started performing the Black Hat Dance. Dress code of the people represented their village and their culture through dance or song or drama they performed. One by one, groups of people started dancing around fire.

I too decided to dance. We all had waited for *Karsha-Gustor* festival for a year. I dragged Yoko and Chime with me and soon we merged with the crowd dancing from the bottom of the heart, swirling, bouncing; mind floating between myth and reality. Father and Maa were watching over us, we blurred in the dusty crowd. Lamas from the *'Bardan'* Monastery joined us.

Lamas dressed in traditional clothes and century old masks with music performed enthralling dance dramas. They manifested guardian spirits.

Evil forces were warded off.

Chime started crying looking at the vibrant colored mask; its red eyes were wide open, and mouth flashing vicious teeth.

Maa calmed her, "Chime, it is Lama behind the mask, this devil is not real."

Taking advantage of her fright I ran after her making scary faces and sounds. I asked the Lama if he could give me the mask . . . without hesitation he handed over the mask to me. It was too heavy for me; Yoko helped me to carry it. Holding the mask we both sat among the crowd to see the performance. Maa with all the other women performed 'Chhams'—a sacred dance, supporting the main character.

It was the day when I could see Maa in her full swing; carefree.

It became a pure 'Buddha'-land and the universe filled with brilliant light of compassionate wisdom manifesting everywhere to awaken all beings.

The celebration ended with delicious 'Khapse'; deep-fried, bite-sized, and twisted pastries. We gorged on the pastries; it was a royal treat. Yoko and I filled our pockets with pastries before anyone could see us.

We rushed home late in the evening. We were already feeling dizzy after dancing like crazy. We reached Yoko's house and I realized that time had come to go away from Yoko. My heart suddenly became heavy. I resigned with a nervous smile. Standing at the door he was staring at me, I turned back to wave; hoping he might wave, hoping to see glimmers of a smile. But he kept his hands behind his back. As the street stretched long, I craned my neck to have a glance at him; Yoko for me was nothing but a dot.

I hung the mask I got from Lama on the wall. I emptied my pockets filled with cakes and packed them in my sack for the next day's journey. We had to start early the next day. Our luggage was ready.

I dashed to the bed. "How devils must be looking like in their real life?" staring at the mask I thought.

I slipped into a dazed and exhausted sleep.

Next morning we woke up with the sound of a gong. That day I saw my Maa first. She had a sleepless night. She simmered water and we freshened up. Father finished milking our yaks. We then drank our *Po-cha*. Mother dropped us till the verandah. She kissed Chime and me. The gentle, caring, maternal expression appeared on her face.

3

JOURNEY BEGINS

Walking through the whitewashed villages, billowing fields of barley we scurried down the rocky canyon to set our first foot on *Chadar*.

The dawn sun lit the Himalayan peaks and clouds with a rosy hue against an azure sky.

Nature had laid thick *Chadar*—the blanket of ice.

People in the valleys could trade and travel till Ladakh for two months. Any moment nature would cease the century old route.

A whole new frozen world could melt soon.

Father poked the ice with his stick; waited for a moment then poked it again which drew a line of satisfaction on his face.

Chime and I were watching Father from a safe distance; his lean figure standing in the middle of the river surrounded by mountains. His body bent down with the luggage he was carrying on his back. Standing on the glassy track he called us, "Chime, Kaba come; it's all safe." His voice more relieved. We both ran towards him balancing ourselves on slippery track.

Chime had first time stepped on *Chadar*. She slipped twice while running.

"Chime, hold me and get up, carefully," extending my hand, firming my feet on icy track I said.

She gripped my hand tightly and dragged me as well on the slippery floor while getting up.

"Thud . . . ." sound echoed in the valley.

We burst into laughter. Father yelled, "Kaba, behave yourself and follow me." I shrugged. Holding Chime I got up.

As he led us forward, he checked each step carefully. He stroked his stick on the ice ahead; making sure the thickness of ice would hold our weight. The ice looked blue but up close it was so clear that walking felt like levitating over the brown river rocks. Tiny cracks and air bubbles suspended within ice signified its presence.

Like a shadow, we were following Father; balancing ourselves with luggage on our back and same time listening to his list of precautions. The same lines that I had been hearing for the last five years: "One wrong step can get us into trouble. If you put your foot anywhere where it's not firm enough it may crack and you will fall into the freezing river. Then you know what happens next."

I knew each line word by word: "If someone falls into the river and doesn't get help quickly, they will survive only for a few minutes. So it is better to be cautious."

He was narrating and behind him I was mimicking, Chime was laughing over this care freely; her laughter as if ice was cracking beneath us. Father finished what he was saying, looked back and asked me astonishingly, "What's the matter, why are you laughing?" I replied, "Father, I have learnt all your precautions by now."

Becoming serious over what I considered small thing, he said, "Stop it and behave."

Then he looked at Chime and said, "Chime, I am saying all this specifically for you, better to be safe than sorry."

We continued walking . . .

I had learned one thing on this trek that the leader tastes integrity of ice with each step. The followers have to mimic the leader but for a leader it is trial and error, high stake game.

After covering few miles we spotted a group of six porters hauling wooden logs. I had always seen porters dragging different size of logs . . .

"Where are they going with this wood, Father?" Chime asked.

"Ladakh market . . . to sell the timber and gain staple in exchange," haltingly, Father said.

"It looks so heavy. How can they travel with such weight?" puzzled Chime uttered.

"Hard work runs in every Zanskari's vein, dear," said Father.

Father waved at a slim-courteous, old man who was leading the porters' group; no one was a stranger in the Zanskar valley.

As we reached closer to the group, a pair of shy, grey eyes bade us welcome with the gentle smile; a flash of recognition crossed his face. He was uncle Tsering.

Uncle Tsering could have been in his sixties but his spirit was as young as any twenty years old man.

His sensitive face sagged with age speaking about the life he led. He had crossed *Chadar* for over thirty years of his life. He was too old to drag the logs but during two harsh months of winter, for livelihood hauling the woods was the only source.

Finding a company during the journey pleased Father. "How are you, uncle?" Father asked uncle Tsering.

"Welcome to the land of *Sharshok*," uncle Tsering uttered joyously, hauling the wood.

Sharshok protects travelers on their journeys over the ice, Zanskaris say.

"I hope, we will reach market safely if *Sharshok* protects us; you know how tough and treacherous it is to haul these logs." Uncle replied dragging the log with all of his strength.

Spirits, demons, beliefs surround world of any Zanskari . . .

Uncle knitted his brow, looking at me uncle said, "So, all set to go to school?"

"Yes uncle. I will be in the fifth grade this year," straightening up head in the air I said. Uncle nodded with appraisal.

"Is this little princess also going to school?" looking at Chime uncle Tsering asked surprisingly.

"Yes Uncle, I am going to School with brother," stroking one of her pigtails behind she replied shyly; her face turned into crimson red.

I knew it was momentary; you spend an hour with her and she would open her chatterbox; shyness never reflected in her.

We traversed the picturesque landscape with hills bathed in gentle apricot light. The alpine and willow trees that we passed by had their green needles hidden under snow, their arms extended open-heartedly, and they had embraced as many flakes as they could.

Following Father we kept on walking and talking. Careful walking didn't mean we needed to be mute.

Chime asked me, "Brother, tell me about the school. Is it big?"

I started describing enthusiastically, "It is bigger than *Karsha* monastery.

"Bigger than *Karsha* monastery?" Chime muttered.

"Yes. Willow, apricot trees and fields surround our school; Indus River runs by our school side." Gasping my breath I further added, "There are two buildings full of classrooms; and an open oval shaped courtyard."

"Courtyard!" Chime exclaimed.

"Yes courtyard! We play during the recess in the courtyard. Near courtyard we have a small assembly hall."

"What do you do there?" another question.

"We pray in the morning at assembly hall and sing National anthem *Jana . . . Gana . . . Mana*. After anthem we head towards respective classrooms in a queue and our P.T. teacher Mr. Zaidi, an old, silver-haired Professor, inspects our uniforms."

Setting my loose bag strap properly on the shoulder I said.

"We call him Captain Zaidi."

"Why Captain?" Chime asked.

"He is very strict. If he finds anyone's uniform or shoes untidy or dirty he punishes us by making us stand outside the classroom for one lecture."

Attentively Father was listening to me.

"Do you remember your first day of school, brother?" Her query came up.

I was struggling hard to gasp breath.

"My first day?" I thought for a moment and continued, "Yes, I remember. I was nervous on my first day of school. I couldn't feel stable at the sight of the building."

Inhaling sharply I further said, "I was not aware Father was going to drop me there . . . Father handed me to the teacher and told me he would come back after his meeting with cheese vendors . . . I was on the brink of tears . . .

I entered classroom hoping Father would return soon. But he never came back. And I broke down in the classroom. I wanted to go back to Zanskar. I thought Father was a heartless man who dropped me at this unknown place." I uttered glancing at Father.

Father's face bore a hint of smile.

"Then, what happened?"

"The class teacher then asked my name and whereabouts. I replied his questions promptly. He patted me on my back. The kindness of teacher soothed my feelings and my nervousness vanished."

I spoke haltingly, "But every teacher is not kind. Professor Charak is annoying."

"Why don't you like him?" our little teacher asked.

"He teaches Math's, and always throws a surprise test. He makes us solve the sum in front of everyone, on the huge blackboard."

"If you study sincerely, you can always solve the sum, Kaba," Father interrupted.

"But Father, he not even throws a test but watches over us holding the wooden ruler, through his round-shaped glasses, which is always on his nose and not on eyes." I answered squirming.

"Hiee . . . hiee . . . hiee . . ." Chime giggled. Father rolled his eyes.

"And if we don't crack the answer right, he thrashes with the wooden ruler and make us kneel down by holding both the ears."

Smile on her face vanished. "Will he teach me too, brother?" nervously Chime asked me.

"Yes. But not this year, Chime." My answered seemed relieved her.

"Do you know what my friend Dorje, Kalsang and I do to avoid Professor Charak's lecture?"

Father stared at me. Chime urged, "Brother, what you do to stay out of the classroom?"

Father continued gazing at me. He expected me not to reveal these ideas to Chime and spoil her. He stopped for a moment, trying to raise his voice he said, "Kaba that is the reason you go to the school for? This is why I am letting you study?" Father was scolding me and Chime was enjoying his gestures.

She interrupted, "Brother, you still haven't told me what you do during Professor Charak's lecture? Please tell me."

Trying to uphold his temper Father said, "Just stop it Chime, this is why . . ." Before he could finish his sentence Chime started laughing. He looked at us sternly. We both suppressed our laughter.

It was fun teasing Father that way. Porters were listening to our conversation; their presence embarrassed Father. He cocked his head other way to hide his expressions; he knew he could never get mad at Chime. When he turned his face we again continued laughing.

We were still walking, there was no horizon; mountains were always in front of us.

A monastery appeared hanging out on the edge of the cliff, clearly outlined in the sky. One Lama was trying to read a thick parchment in the sun. Every time I tried looking for trail heading upwards but couldn't find any. Ancient villages peppered the valleys between the passes. Smoke curled into the air from flat roofs of the village homes. Few monks were meditating beneath the open sky. Soothing calmness in the atmosphere was making my *Chadar* journey more soulful.

We walked through the walls of the Zanskar canyon twist and turn; sometimes we passed through narrow passage . . . Sometimes those passages spread out to make the flat white *Chadar* seemed wider than a football field. Father was carrying a wooden cart. When he found the surface flat and slippery he tied the cart with a rope, loaded it with our luggage and started dragging it by tying the other end of the rope around his chest.

After covering few miles he carried the luggage on his back.

"Sit on the cart, Chime," he stated.

Chime hurriedly settled on the cart; Father started pulling it.

"Yiee . . . yiee," she yelled, her chirpy voice bounced in the valley. Chime was thoroughly enjoying it; she never had experienced anything like this.

I was eagerly waiting for my turn. Walking was consuming almost all of my breath.

"Chime, let your brother sit for a while. He is tired," Father said. Unwillingly Chime got up and allowed me to sit. Father was dragging me as if I was nothing but wool. Every drag pulled his muscles.

The porters were hauling their timber.

The walk was exhausting. Father asked, "Chime, are you hungry?"

Chime said, "Yes Father, I am hungry." Father asked uncle Tsering, "Uncle, should we halt for lunch?"

Uncle nodded with approval; with porters we Offloaded the luggage underneath the protrude cliff and sat for a while gasping breath. We drank water from our filled water bottles. Father then asked me to open the Tiffin.

Porters set fire; within minutes they had tea boiling over a roaring driftwood fire. I reached my sack and removed aluminum Tiffin. Chime, bending on her knees was greedily looking at the Tiffin; waiting for me to open it.

Uncle Tsering dipped his finger in his cup, flickered some tea to the sky. "For *Sharshok*," he said ironically and all porters continued with their lunch.

Maa had packed my favorite *'momos'*-steamed dumplings stuffed with herbs. The aroma increased my appetite and I couldn't wait anymore to eat it. I didn't wish to share *momos* with anyone. Together we dung our hands in Tiffin. I took small bites, nibbling the edges until the filled center is left, and then finally popped the last precious morsel into mouth. *Momos* were delicious. I missed Maa while eating.

Eating food, beneath the open sky was my favorite thing.

I shared *Khapse* with Chime and porters I had got from monastery the other night. Uncle Tsering enjoyed the pastries most; I felt glad I packed them.

We rested for a while.

Uncle said, "Let's leave Norbu. We must move on without wasting time. Before sunset we have to find a safe shelter." Father agreed with him.

Wrapping the sack Father said, "Kaba, Chime collect your bags. We must start walking."

We endured our journey on the corridor of ice. Few hours passed while walking, we came across a frozen waterfall. It was descending from a cliff below; a waterfall that looked like human nose. One tunnel, water froze; the other tunnel was dry!!

Amazed by the waterfall sight, Chime asked, "Father, why this waterfall is dry at one end?"

Listening to her question uncle Tsering spoke, "Dear, do you want to know the story behind it?"

Stories always fascinated Chime. She replied, "Yes uncle, off course!!"

Uncle while walking, dragging the timber said, "Years ago in the remote village in Zanskar Valley, there was a powerful astrologer. The village was suffering from scarcity of water for irrigation since ages. The astrologer, in his effort helped out the people, went to Tibet to meet the head Lama for help. That repeated a few good numbers of times till they decided to help the astrologer. They gave him a box and asked him to carry it to his village. They also warned him not to open the box till he reaches his place. Happy with his success, the astrologer started."

"What did he carry in the box?" Chime questioned.

Touching her chubby cheeks tenderly, uncle continued, "The closer he was reaching to his village, heavier the box was getting. And so was his curiosity about what was there inside the box . . . like yours" he added.

"Then what happened uncle?" I asked inquisitively.

"When he was hardly a couple of hours from the village, his curiosity forced him to open the box. The moment he opened the box, two big fishes jumped out of the box." Chime was carefully listening to him.

Gasping for the breath he continued, "The two fishes hit at two separate places a few miles up in the rocks and penetrated the mountain. They penetrated the rock and made a tunnel till *'Tsomo Lake'*, a large lake in Tibet. The fishes reached the lake and water started flowing through the tunnel."

"Such a fool the astrologer was!" I interrupted.

"Yes, he realized his mistake. Had he opened the box in his village, the fishes would have made a tunnel from his village to *'Tsomo'* and they could solve water scarcity. The sad astrologer went back to the village. He tried his best to divert the tunnel to the village, in vain. In his effort, he had closed one of the tunnels."

"Remember my child, 'patience' in life plays important role," Uncle quoted.

Story engrossed us and made our journey easier. Vivid orange sunset had lit up the sky turning the *Chadar* into red carpet . . . we were walking on it like guests in the palace marveling at the beauty around us. Cold wind racked the ranges.

Father was looking for the alpine trees; same place we halted every year. Though I knew the path I always depended on my Father's skill and experience to cross the *Chadar*. I could never understand how every time Father managed to locate those trees in puzzled route. We continued walking looking for alpines. And from a distance we could see the silhouettes of the trees leaning towards golden skyline.

The moment we went closer it felt like heaven. The view was alluring! It was dusk; partly sunlight and partly moonlight fell on the trees between the white colored snow mountains. Father chose that place for our night halt because there he could easily get some wood to keep us warm. Chime and I settled near one alpine tree. We dumped our luggage.

Getting rid off his luggage Father said, "Children, do you know gravels and coarse sand dominates alpine soil, surface nearby these trees is hard enough to rest. And we can always climb on these trees if wild animal arrives looking for his dinner." Chime started laughing at Father's poor joke.

I was always scared of wild animals; even thinking of them gave me goose bumps. Luckily we had a company of porters.

Exhausted by carrying heavy woods all day long porters too settled with us. They disburdened their stuff and started preparing dinner. Father rested for few minutes. Before dark, he decided to arrange some wood for the fire. Hurriedly getting up he made a firm grip around the tree and started climbing. He reached the middle of the tree within few minutes; one by one he cut off few branches. Chime was watching Father in awe. She never saw Father climb on the tree.

She yelled, "Father, be careful. You will fall." Looking her worried face Father started laughing. He came down slowly and said, "Look, I didn't fall." Chime grinned. I collected all the branches; with Father I broke them into pieces. Chime too tried to break the branches with her soft hands. Father lit the fire with the help of the branches.

First day of the journey had emptied our water bottles, we were all thirsty. Father collected the upper layer of ice, filled the container and placed on the fire to melt. We drank some water and filled the rest in our bottles. Father refilled the container with ice for some more water. Then he cooked *'skiu'* a starch—based dish that looks like an ear-shaped pasta and spiced vegetables. It was always during our *Chadar* journey I saw him cooking, my Maa never allowed him to cook when at home.

Chime and I kept adding wood to the fire to fuel it and kept poking it. We tried to warm ourselves as best as we could. When we faced the fire, the wind would come from behind us, freezing the backside. Porters then cooked *'tsampa'*—a doughy paste of roasted barley combined with yak-butter tea; a high-energy staple in our region. We perched around the bonfire, shared our dinner with porters. Plunged in her two fingers, Chime made a hearty meal.

I laid all three sleeping bags; we went to the bed underneath the sky. A full moon had climbed up a quarter of the sky, silence had spread its wing over the earth, the mountains deepened in blue, cold and indifferent; the fire was still burning.

4

ENCHANTING MANTRAS

$\mathcal{B}$eneath a frigid dawn, wind was playing mischievously; it was still dark. *Bong-bong* of the gong was missing but Father woke up as usual. He woke Chime and me up. We freshened up and packed our bags.

Father lit a small lantern showing us the path. We were trailing, followed by the porters; the light source of the lantern was bouncing on the crystal blue icy floor creating sparkling rays. With every footstep, Father was checking firmness of the ice with his stick. A few hours passed, the first ray of the sunlight hit the peak of the mountain washing it in soft pink and saffron. Father switched off the lantern to save the fuel for emergency.

Chadar is so magical and mysterious; every turn we were taking had something new to offer. Every view was breathtaking. Nature was changing its costume every hour. Flaunting marvelous collection it possessed, leaving us spellbound.

Chadar journey was never about walking on the ice, it was always an experience of feeling nature's beauty at extreme conditions. As long as we were walking we tended to stay warm. But if we stopped even for a moment—20 degrees would hit us with a bang. Our hand could go numb if not protected properly.

Within just a few miles of comfortable walking the forlorn beauty transformed into something malicious. The heavy snow weighed on already unstable ice; *Chadar* was melted. One more step ahead and we could be beneath the ice.

Father warned, "Chime, Kaba, just stop. Don't move even by an inch." He looked around for safe way; unfortunately there was not any other way. The only possible way was melted. He dropped the cheese container and luggage on the icy floor and moved forward stealthily, holding his pajamas upwards. He dipped his stick in the water to check the depth of the river; it was knee-deep.

Grabbing our sacks with the luggage and cheese container, he got into the freezing cold water. His thin body suppressed with the burden of luggage, with his every step the ice was cracking underneath.

Crossing the river he reached the other side, the ground was firm and stable. Father dropped everything there on the hard surface and started walking up to us. He picked me and Chime both on his shoulder and crossed the icy path again.

Porters floated their timber in the river and started walking, pulling the logs simultaneously. They waded through the freezing cold water barefoot to reach the shelter dry. By the time we reached on the firm surface Father was all wet. Water filled his boots, soaked his pajamas. He removed his shoes to empty them. His one shoe had hole; it emptied naturally.

Chime got a new pair of socks from the sack and said, "Father wear these." Her concern surprised Father. He wore the fresh pair of socks. We felt need of fire to warm ourselves. Porters cut some wood pieces out of the logs and lit the fire. Everyone was shivering after getting wet in the icy river. We dried Father's socks, shoes over the fire. Father was rubbing his hands to keep himself warm. Tea was boiling over the fire; its aroma awakened our senses.

Uncle Tsering said sadly, "When I first started walking on the *Chadar* forty years ago, the ice was various levels deep. You fall through one or two layers, ice would be still underneath, and the bottom layer would remain unbreakable. And now, a single misstep plunges a traveler beneath a layer."

One porter poured tea into cups for everyone. The other porter began speaking about the twenty-two years old porter Jungney who had died previous year.

"Jungney had been pulling a sled with a rope wrapped around his hand when the sled fell through the ice and dragged him under," said the porter.

"A real misfortune, he had children too," Uncle said.

After having refreshing tea; we set ourselves further. We carried our sacks and luggage; porters loaded their logs of wood.

Uncle Tsering was leading us all. We were following him with other porters. We came across the sacred stone; '*Om Mani Padme Hum*' carved on it. Uncle started reciting '*Om Mani Padme Hum*'. All other porters started repeating the mantra in chorus after uncle finished his.

I joined all the porters in chorus chanting the mantra. Seeing me enjoying the mantra, Chime tried to recite it, but beyond '*Om Mani*' she couldn't pronounce the *Sanskrit* words. Dedicatedly she kept murmuring, "*Om Mani . . . Om Mani . . .*"

I had listened mantra many times while crossing the *Chadar* trek so was familiar.

During my first journey on *Chadar* Father had told me that saying the Mantra loud or even silently invokes the powerful benevolent attention and blessings of '*Chenerzig*'—the embodiment of compassion.

We kept walking repeating mantra several times . . .

While walking Father was talking to uncle, "Today, commercial butter is available in the market about quarter price of our yak butter. I have to really work hard to maintain its quality and high fat or else it would be difficult to make money." Worry reflected in his words.

Further we reached towards a narrow passage; the mist blue fog draped river was singing its song, to the heart of listening earth. It was the place where *Chadar* never freezes.

It was a strange view . . . the frozen waterfall hung with icicles on its edges, on the contrary the river was flowing. I was awestruck by the wonder of nature's fury.

The giant granite, sandstone canyon walls were watching over us. To cross the *Chadar* further, few 'U' shaped metal rods were inserted in canyon walls everyone had to pass metal rods while crossing *Chadar*; it was part of our journey.

Porter group was ahead of us. They tied wooden logs with a rope and held the edge of the rope in the hand. One by one, with each other's help they crossed the path. After crossing the metal rods, they got down on a firm ground and pulled the log towards them. This way, it took them more than an hour to cross the rock over metal rods. One of the young porters dropped his logs on the other side, he came back and held uncle Tsering's wooden log and crossed the rods again.

Three of us and Uncle Tsering were left to cross the river through the U shape metal rods. Uncle Tsering headed us; Father put his first feet carefully on the rods, carrying luggage and cheese containers. He moved a step ahead, clambered up the canyon walls like a lizard. As he reached midway he stretched his hand towards Chime and said, "Chime, hold my hand and place your right foot on the rod at the same time."

In the beginning Chime was hesitant to move ahead; she stood still, those rods were thin and slippery. She was staring at them, horrified. Father said, "Come on dear, move ahead, give me your hand, you have to just follow me step by step. Don't worry . . . I will not let you fall, just look at me and walk . . ."

I uttered, "Go Chime, don't worry. I do it every year. It's easy." Back of my mind I knew I was scared too; though I crossed it every year. Chime lifted her right foot; shakily placed it on the rod, in a moment as she looked down, she withdrew herself back.

Uncle Tsering cheered from the other side to boost her confidence, "You can do it. You are a strong girl of Zanskar . . . don't be afraid, cross it and make us feel proud."

All the other porters started yelling, "Come Chime . . . come on . . . you are a brave girl."

Father was trying to maintain a balance between Chime and the luggage he was carrying. The strap of his cheese container was slipping from his right shoulder, He was struggling hard to weigh his cheese container and at the same time to hold Chime. I knew he couldn't afford loosing the cheese; it was his whole year's earnings.

Chime finally extended her foot carefully; placing left hand on the rocky wall of the canyon she stretched her right hand towards Father. He pulled Chime towards him cautiously carrying the heavy load on right shoulder. With Chime's every footstep Father moved one step behind. One wrong step could cost either his life or Chime's. I was watching them nervously. They slithered on the firm ledge. With Chime's first step on the safe surface uncle Tsering and other porters lifted her . . . they all patted her back. Chime crossed the hurdle; it relieved Father.

I guess Chime was the youngest girl who was crossing the *Chadar*. Crossing such a hurdle could be an achievement, for girl as young as Chime. Finally, my turn arrived. Father kept his luggage and cheese container on the safer ground and climbed those rods back towards me to give me a hand. Chime, being younger to me had crossed the path. I couldn't display my fear.

"Cross the path, stupid. Your pride is at stake; porters will call you a coward if you would not cross." My subconscious murmured. I gave my hand to Father and crossed the metal ledges swiftly.

Standing on a sloping ledge of the canyon I could see swirling mists and cliffs rising into the clouds; it was a passage to another world . . . a paradise.

We continued further; wasting time could cost us a day; that means delay in delivery of cheese for Father. About an hour of pure adrenaline rushed over the snow and boulders to the pass left us gushing.

But *Chadar* had several challenges to offer; almost after two hours of walk we stumbled upon a new challenge. It was a narrow bend, '*Woma*'. *Woma* pass was not frozen.

Uncle Tsering said sarcastically, "Now the only way to get across is with wings."

Chadar was feeble there; the power of nature that had stopped the flow of once playful, treacherous river flabbergasted me. It could shatter like a glass any moment we step on it.

Father looked around, he shuffled his eyes, on our right side was a high canyon wall; the only way forward was to ascend the steep wall of the gorge.

Uncle Tsering's face darkened. He spoke disappointedly, "Norbu, with heavy logs of wood, there is no hope for us to climb. We might wait until this river freezes."

"I can understand uncle, to travel with logs will be perfidious; but I must leave. I need to deliver the cheese," Father said.

He paused and said, " Norbu, wait till tonight, if the *Chadar* doesn't freeze till tomorrow morning, you can continue your journey; but if it forms we all will go together. It will please me to travel with you further; children will be safe in a group . . . I love their company."

It was fun walking with the porters, reciting the mantra in chorus; it motivated us to keep moving. Chime requested innocently, "Please Father, let's stay back with uncle Tsering . . . please."

The last light of day tinted the air and earth. It was possible to walk few more miles but we decided to slow down and based near the mountain. We took off our bags and sat underneath the ledge overhang of the glacier.

Chime and I sat near uncle. Some thoughts engaged uncle Tsering. His wrinkled face was speaking about his worry. Father noticed uncle's uneasiness; he asked, "What is the matter, uncle? You look lost. I don't believe that was you who cheered up for Chime some time back."

Staring deep into the flowing river uncle spoke seriously, recollecting his thoughts, "Over the last four decades, the average winter temperatures have steadily climbed in the region . . . making the *Chadar* ice less and less stable. One day when the path completely vanishes, *Sharshok*, the demons and protectors, the myths and the legends, will vanish too." His concern for his valley, for Mother Earth reflected through his narrow eyes. His mouth set in a hard, grim line.

Chokingly he said, "Our Mother Earth belongs to no one and she belongs to us all. We should cherish her . . . instead we are destroying her . . . the warming temperature is a result of our spiritual failings. We have become too materialistic, Norbu." He was speaking like a monk.

A ubiquitous white noise of the rushing river overlapped his words.

There was no source of firewood around to light the bonfire; one porter lit the stove.

They couldn't cut the wooden logs all through their journey for fire; those logs were going to pay them, and the only source of their yearly income . . . much less than the efforts they took.

They always carried either dung or portable stove to save wood. As the stove lit, porter prepared tea. We drank it together. All the porters with each other's help cooked gravy like dish mixing some rice and herbs together. Father helped them to cook the dish; he gave them some cheese to add to the gravy for richer flavor. They shared their food with us generously. Our second night passed without opening our Tiffin. We were eating freshly cooked food . . . We were fortunate. Dinning under a star-studded sky, amidst the high hilly ranges, in an open was truly a wonderful experience.

The night advanced as the moon brightened the land, but in its stark light cold slipped between the folds. With some more uncle Tsering's bedtime stories Chime and I went to sleep.

5

GOOD LUCK CHARM

Unwrinkled sheet of blue was glowing in the first rays of dawn, still frangible.

"I can't stay back one more day, we must climb the rock." Father said.

Uncle Tsering tried to divert Father's mind; he said, "Norbu, I am not feeling confident about you journeying further on this shatter able *Chadar*. Let it take its time, what is the hurry? We always prefer to wait, sometimes that takes three days to four days; you know well how restless its free spirit is."

But Father was determined about his decision that day, he didn't agree with uncle. He said convincingly, "Uncle I need to enroll Chime in the school, it will take much time. I need to deliver the cheese to vendors; they must be waiting. I am running out of time. I can't afford to wait for one more day, please allow me to proceed further."

Uncle Tsering replied, "I wish I could have joined you and climbed the rock but my old age doesn't allow me."

We filled our bottles with water, loaded sacks on our shoulder. All the porters said goodbye to us, wishing us luck for our further journey uncle said, "Norbu, if *Chadar* gets firm soon then we would try to catch you ahead. If we don't catch up ahead we would meet you in the timber market. After dropping the kids to school, come to the market, we will return together."

Father assured, "I will certainly come over and if we are lucky, we will get some trekkers. We can guide them and earn some money."

Time arrived . . . we had to depart.

Uncle Tsering would no longer accompany us; the fact saddened me.

Uncle said thoughtfully, "My father had told me; the restless spirits of the river will try to kill you once. However, if you survive . . . walking the *Chadar* will certainly be the most stunning journey you will ever make." He always harbored positive thoughts.

Uncle looked at Chime; reaching to his *goncha* pocket he removed something. Bending on his knees he said lovingly, "Chime, my dear, give me your hand."

Puzzled Chime extended her hand. Uncle placed one shiny, red stone on her palm. "Keep this coral. It will protect you from the evil eye; will give you strength and bring you good fortune to begin your school life. I always carry this good luck charm with me . . . now it's all yours," he uttered warmly, planting a kiss on her forehead.

Uncle recited, "*Om Mani Padme Hum*"; we chanted, "*Om Mani Padme Hum*" and continued our journey.

Muscular peaks were towering us. Physical and mental challenge stood in front of us.

Porter Kalden was all ready to help us.

I had never climbed a rock, such a big rock before. It was I think fifteen-twenty meter. One wrong step could have meant broken bones else straight down the Zanskar. Challenge terrified me.

Father loaded his luggage; hung his cheese container on right shoulder and tightened its strap.

"Chime, climb up on my back," he commanded. Porter Kalden helped Chime to climb up on Father's shoulder. She clutched Father tightly. Father waved at uncle Tsering, "See you soon, uncle," he yelled. Uncle nodded.

Father extended his right hand and left foot . . . then left foot and right hand . . . synchronizing . . . like a lizard. Finding the holes and gaps on the rock he was ascending so swiftly as if he had done it several times. Chime had tightened her grip around Father's neck; her eyes closed; face blood red. With his every move he was checking his cheese container. Only feet left to reach to the top of the rock, Father started panting; the more he was moving forward, the heavier it became. He was struggling to find the grip.

Porter Kalden shouted, "There, there . . . just above your right hand . . . stretch your left leg." I was twisting my fingers, praying for his safety. My heart was pounding; my breathing shallowed.

Gathering his entire courage and strength Father touched the top of the cliff and in a moment he was standing on the top; Chime, still on his back, waving at me. I waved back to her.

I breathed deeply. My subconscious was bucking me up, "You are not afraid of height. No other option!!! You must climb."

Father yelled from the top, "You must do it Kaba . . . there's no point in thinking anything. At point like this, fear doesn't help."

I readied myself. Porter Kalden subsequently started guiding me. "Use your foot power only from the fingers, and it will all become easier," he advised me.

I struggled to maintain the grip and to find gaps, I couldn't advance further, some of the points were tricky and tips of the fingers started to hurt. I was just hoping to find some gap. "Kaba, just above your left side, there is a gap. Move further a little, you are almost there." He was encouraging me. He knew too well where the gaps were; his skinny frame would fool anyone. Plastered to the wall made it difficult to find holes and gaps.

There was a small extension at one place. It was barely one foot wide and three feet long.

Porter Kalden directed, "Keep your left foot on the extension and extend your right hand." I breathed several times before extending my foot. I wished I could fly instead. My arms started to tremble, my legs worn out.

When I stretch too hard, a muscle in one of my legs suddenly stiffen to the point it hurt quite a bit.

I climbed what seemed to be a great distance, and decided to look down. There was nothing below me, only the swirling gusts of wind. I was in a daze; it was exhilarating.

I climbed till eternity.

Father, standing on the top commanded, " Kaba, extend your hand towards me." I chanted, " *Om Mani Padme Hum*" and extended my hand towards Father above; setting my foot on an extended portion I felt a good grip on the extension, just below the joint of my toe. This boosted my confidence. One more step and I knew I would be in safe hands. Father pulled me up by holding my hand from above. My elbows reached the surface of the rock; I climbed up with the help of my hands!

Some time back, I was just standing at the bottom of this rock wall, fixing my climbing harness, thinking whether I would make it. But when I did, I felt a sense of accomplishment.

The rock was flat and bare on the way up. The view was spectacular. Porters were cheering for me.

Porter Kalden threw a rope towards Father; He held it tight along with other porters.

Father held the rope and carefully started descending to the other side of the rock. Every step took me closer to the ground. I found it relatively easy; I had to follow Father.

When we touched the ground, the whole world was under my feet. It was really tiring; my limbs started to ache. Finally, after two hours, we successfully tackled the hurdle. Father released the rope; as he did, our contact with porters loosened.

The majestic limestone rock was looking down on us; morning reddish rays of the rising sun began to strike it.

Walking for half of the day, after the treacherous journey we waited for lunch. This time porters were not with us, I missed uncle Tsering. We opened our Tiffin and had our food.

Father relaxed on his sleeping bag and reenergized himself to continue the rest of the journey.

Sitting on the banks of the river, I was observing explosion of colors.

A thought sprung in my mind, "Maa would be spinning wool this hour of the day seated on verandah. I know she would sew new silver—grey fur coat for me. She had promised me, when I will reach home from school, I will get fur coat."

I was rendering my thoughts "Once I would become a teacher I would not let Father work hard. He wouldn't have to make cheese and travel all the way to Ladakh every year."

I was eagerly waiting to finish my school; all my plans were ready . . .

A marmot jumped in front of me disturbing my dreams. Chime was running after marmot to catch it. Marmot was teasing her . . . jumping from one place to other . . . halting in between the snowy rocks . . . whistling. The moment Chime reached close, it ran away finding its way through rocks. Father saw restless Chime wandering around. He warned her, "Chime, you better sit down if you really wish to go to the school, or else I would leave you behind, and take Kaba along with me." Listening to Father's threat, Chime quietly slid by my side.

With renewed energy, we followed the remaining trail. We came to a further narrowing; ice blocks were floating on the way.

We walked through the gorges of varying depths and widths; a lot of snow had fallen on the narrow gorges. We reached at the terrifying ice ledge; the ledge was barely three feet wide, heavily covered with snow. There was a ten-meter drop to the flowing river below.

Every bend tested his skill; at every twist and turn of the valley he had to prove how good a father he was. His courage truly was like Himalaya; protecting us from all worldly danger. Father said, "Children, follow me.

Just do the way I do. Remember, whatever happens, don't get panic."

He perched on one and half feet wide icy ledge, crawling. Only one person could crawl the ledge at a time. Father was testing sturdiness of the ledge with his stick before moving ahead to make sure it would not fall down. When he reached at the center of the ledge, without looking back he said, "Chime, follow me. Use leg power . . . more than arm power, and keep as close to the wall as possible. Crawl slowly." Father slithered on safer ground.

Chime started sliding on the ledge; when she reached at the center, she stopped. Father yelled, "Chime, don't stop . . . it's not safe, move ahead." After Chime, I slid on the ledge. I had crawled that ledge in the past. I followed Chime, pushing my elbows on icy surface, stretching my legs. My sight went down, Zanskar River was roaring below; a chill ran down my spine. Halting at one place was dangerous; it could break due to prolonged pressure. Cautiously I slid and reached the safer ground.

As I got down, Chime exclaimed, "Look behind," her eyes were dancing with excitement.

I turned back to see why Chime was so thrilled!

In the blaze of sunshine, thousands of rainbows appeared, as a thousand rainbow rings, swaying in and out of existence with the wind and the gravity of their fall . . . Leaping, bouncing off the frozen *Chadar* onto the canyon walls in a kaleidoscope of colors.

The unparalleled beauty of the valley was stunning. Was that an enigmatic land the best painting done by God ever? I had never noticed so many forms, so many shades of *Chadar* before.

I often travelled with Father, he was always in a hurry to cross the path and reach the destination. I was now, looking at the nature through Chime's perspective.

That day Chime was with me, and I was enjoying the journey with her. Walking on *Chadar* was like venturing on the land of GOD. Chime was just five; hence she was unaware of menacing *Chadar* and free from all types of tensions. She was always relaxed and in a playful mood. I experienced a totally different view of *Chadar* that time.

It was always monotonous walk with Father. His only target on the journey was to reach on time; deliver the cheese in the market without any delay, buy the staple and reach home safe before *Chadar* melts.

Whenever I stopped I could hear Father saying, "Come on Kaba, keep walking. You can't stop viewing the nature. We need to cover a very long distance."

Chadar has a nature to keep changing every hour. It changes inexplicably.

We kept walking . . . Chime was exhausted; I slowed down. We had covered a long distance; we were thirsty and dehydrated. We had lost lots of energy in crawling and clambering.

We couldn't lift ourselves up onto the ice, the throbbing in our fingers faded, and our hands no longer seemed as if our own.

"When are we going to stop, Father? I can't lift my feet any more," Chime whispered.

"As soon as we find a safe place, we will halt, dear . . . please, bear with me for some more time," Father replied worriedly.

"I need some water," Chime said, she was panting. Our bottles were empty. It was a hectic day; we walked through the glacial valleys looking for the shelter. The land was barren . . . there was no trail . . . no route.

Towering Himalaya guarded the frozen *Chadar* . . . we were moving along with her bend.

After a little exploration appeared a spring of fresh water . . . it was streaming; attuned with blowing wind. I immediately had a quick sip of water; filled the bottle for Chime, she guzzled it. I refilled our bottles for further journey.

The icy path led us towards a cave. Father was relieved to find the cave. Tall alpine trees loomed on either side; sun filtered white through the snow-capped canopy of leaves.

We marched further; the cave was as if a mysterious eye in the canyon; a meditating eye that watched us enchantingly.

Fiery sky silently ushered evening into the lonely land. The sun was setting down beyond the canyons of Zanskar; the cave, bathed in vermillion hues, hypnotized me. I could see nothing but a cave; it was inviting me on my every step warm-heartedly.

I had crossed the route past four years, but the strange thing is I could never notice this cave. It was mesmerizing . . .

6

MYSTERIOUS CAVE

The cave was charismatic; unlike other caves this cave had a wide entrance, wide enough to shelter fifty people at a time. Lustrous ice layered the entrance reflecting amber rays of the setting sun.

We stood at the entrance, impatiently. Father entered the cave passing through the pits and breakdowns. Creepy silence spread around.

After a while, Father called, "Kaba, Chime come inside . . . watch your step while walking." His voice echoed.

Holding Chime's hand I entered the cave; the path of the cave turned to the right. The darkness enveloped me in never ending fortress of mystic. I could hear a soft dripping noise as dew slid off the rocks. My breathing slowed as I tried inhaling humid air. In the darkness . . . Father kept his luggage down and lit the lamp. Warm, yellow glow of lamp highlighted rough cave walls. Inside, the cave was entirely different; algae had placed its emerald green carpet all over the places. The cave was separated in two parts, yet it didn't change the floors between two areas. I wondered where the other part of the cave leading; it looked eerie.

Dirt was littered everywhere. Left over ash layered the pebbled floor; whoever had sheltered before us had left the garbage behind. "It is not an ideal place to stay but it will keep us warm and save us from night's dropping temperature" I thought.

We found a better corner to arrange our luggage. "Kaba, clean the cave and make some room. I am getting some wood for fire." Father uttered exiting the cave.

I scanned the cave to find something to clean the cave, some paper, some cloth, anything. Luckily, I found a rag lying down in one corner. I started sweeping the floor lazily. The surface of the cave was uneven, pebbly; life chiseled from limestone. "Mother Earth must have taken eons to create this cave," I assumed.

I looked around for Chime; she had made herself comfortable in that creepy space. Seated on one of the rocks, she leaned towards the floor; gazing something attentively. Carrying container I went out to get some ice. It had snowed; so I collected first layer of powdered snow, so we could melt the snow and drink the water. Every passing moment was getting colder and colder.

I reached inside the cave with ice; I heard Chime talking. "In this dark cave whom she is talking? She must have made new friends as usual," I wondered.

Curiously, I walked up to her to see whom she was talking to. I was surprised by what I saw. A beautiful formation of small ants encircled around Chime's finger; she was playing with them, placing her finger on their path. Hundreds of those tiny creatures were forming rectangular shapes, sometimes stars; sometimes circle; in a disciplined manner, without breaking their unity.

I thought, "How can they really do it? In school we students find it difficult to form a straight line; whenever we stood for prayers in queue, it twisted at some point." I was amused to see ant formation; I placed my finger in their path along with Chime excitedly. She grinned.

Chime asked them, "Are you hungry?" She was acting like their mother. She cocked her head towards me and said, "Kaba, these kids must be feeling hungry; we must find food for them." She was so engrossed that she forgot her tiredness. She was back to her energetic spirit.

It was her favorite game. She often used to feed our yaks at home; regardless they are hungry or not.

She examined the cave with her squinty eyes, shifting her glance from one corner to other. I followed her to show my presence in her game. And she yelled pointing at the ceiling of the cave, "Brother, look up there."

I noticed an army of ants marching upwards to eat lush green algae. I blinked up at Chime; her lips twitched in a smile.

"How will you reach there?" Chime asked. Though the ceiling was not so high, I needed some support to reach to the algae.

"I will climb up on that," pointing at one rock I said. Chime grinned.

Placing the left foot on the rock I stretched my right hand towards the ceiling, balancing on one leg.

"Be careful brother," worried Chime alerted me.

Holding my foot on the rock, cautiously, I scrubbed the algae with a piece of sharp stone. It felt like wet wool. Chime carefully cupped her hands to hold the algae; but it slipped through her fingers many times.

She was happy to find food for her friends. Leaning towards the ants we both fed them. One by one ants gathered around the piece of algae; forming a flower shape. Chime was delighted.

Father's presence disturbed our game. "Kaba, Chime, what are you doing in that corner? Come, Help me out here," he said.

He entered with dry wood; I helped him to cut the wood and light the fire. Father said, "Remove your shoes, socks and gloves. They must be wet with moisture." Ice was melting in a pot, on fire. My sweater smelt damp, so as Chime's. We both changed our socks and gloves; I placed them on the rock to let them dry. Outside darkness froze.

Father asked, "Do you want to eat '*skiu*' for dinner?" We both made faces; we were in no mood to have *skiu*. We could save it for further journey.

"Father, can you cook pulses and rice?" I hesitantly asked. He paused staring at me, then said smiling, "Yes, if you help me."

Chime was excited to taste Father's cooked pulses and rice. Maa had taught very little about cooking to Chime. She decided to help Father. I washed pulses and rice. Father filtered the melted water with '*malmal*—cotton cloth.

"What should I do?" restless Chime asked.

Giving her small wooden pieces Father said, "Sweetheart, you feed this fire to keep it alive; so we can cook our food faster." His answer didn't satisfy her.

"I want to cook food with you, Father," Chime pleaded.

"Not now Chime, some other day; let me cook, we all are hungry," Father uttered.

Unwillingly, she sat on her knees near the fire, adding wooden pieces one by one, watching it carefully. Fire erupted, illuminating the cave. Father placed a small container, added rice, pulses and '*masala*'—mixed powdered spices to it. We were tired and hungry; but cooking on a bonfire was fun experience. Steam rose from the container; Father stirred it once to check the consistency. Our dinner was ready.

Chime was eager to taste Father's cooked food; he served the hot and steamy food on plates. Chime burnt her finger when she reached to taste the food. Her delicate pink finger turned red. Food was not great as few spices were missing but we were so hungry the taste of the food really didn't matter to us.

Fire was still burning to keep us warm. After dinner it was time for bedtime stories. I unrolled the sleeping bags.

"Father, can I sleep in the middle?" Sleepily Chime asked.

"Chime is scared, Chime is scared . . ." I yelled, teasing her.

"Stop teasing her Kaba and go to bed," Father snapped. I shrugged and went to the bed thinking how bias Father was.

Chime opened her chatterbox, "Father, who made this cave?"

Father faced a challenging question; collecting his thoughts he said, "Mother Earth." He answered confidently.

"Who is Mother Earth? Does she live here?" her query extended further. I fumed at her; I knew I would have a sleepless night. I was half dead when I fell on the bed.

Father continued, "When '*Siddhartha Gautama*' was seeking enlightenment; demon '*Mara*' attacked him with armies of monsters to frighten him from his seat under the '*Bodhi*' Tree . . .

"Who was '*Siddhartha Gautama*'?" Chime interrupted curiously.

"Lord '*Buddha*' . . . he was '*Siddhartha*' then." Father's answer didn't satisfy Chime.

Father continued, "Though '*Mara*' tried to frighten '*Siddhartha*', he didn't move. Angry '*Mara*' claimed the seat of enlightenment for himself, saying his spiritual accomplishments were greater than *Siddhartha's*. *Mara's* monstrous soldiers cried out together, "I am his witness!" '*Mara*' challenged '*Siddhartha*'—who will speak for you?

"What happened next?" rising on her elbow, exasperated Chime questioned.

"Then '*Siddhartha*', simply touched the ground in response and as the earth cracked and quaked . . . the Goddess of the Earth burst from the grass and soil, wringing waters of the glades from her hair." Gesturing hands in the air Father was talking.

She roared, "I bear you witness!" '*Mara*' disappeared. And as the morning star rose in the sky, '*Siddhartha Gautama*' realized enlightenment and became '*Buddha*'."

He said, "*Lord Buddha* depended on the Mother Earth to testify on his behalf."

"But why did he chose her?" asked sleepless Chime.

"He invoked her because she was the truest, the most reliable witness." Chime grinned at his answer.

"What does she do?" Her eyes briefly shut; but her mouth was entirely open. I was twisting and turning off in my bed.

"She teaches us about supporting life, connectedness and beauty. She is adorned with heights, slopes, plains, hills, mountains, forests, plants, treasures, herbs . . . she takes care of every creature that breathes and stirs . . . she gives us joy, wealth, prosperity, good fortune and glory."

Father kept on talking, spiritually. Chime had already dossed off in his arms. His words faded, I slept soundly.

After couple of hours I woke up; it was windy. Darkness penetrated the earth. Fire almost cooled down. Father drew blanket over Chime. He added some more wood to the dead fire.

"Kaba, watch over for a while. I am going out for a nature's call," he said. Snuggling in the bed I nodded.

He stayed glued to the floor for some reason; his eyes wide open. I found his gesture weird.

"Father, what happened?" I asked. He didn't move.

"Shhh . . . keep quiet . . ." he murmured.

I got up to see what made Father freeze. We caught glimpses of twinkling eyes in the coal dark night; I poked my eye sockets with my fingers . . .

The boundless darkness lurked in the mountains; the tilting alpine, willow trees set the backdrop.

The moments caught my attention. The shapes emerged through the trees and leaped out.

"What is it, Father?" I could hardly get words out.

Before our senses could work, we heard screeching roars. The black objects were walking side by side . . .

then we heard complex series of grunts, varying in pitch and intensity.

We were completely blown up. Father stepped back in shock and collapsed on his back, producing loud, resonating sound. Chime woke up with the thud . . .

Somewhere beyond our comfort zone, they were hunting; terror and death ruled out on the dark. Powerful shapes were prowling . . .

"Snow leopards . . ." Father uttered fumbling.

Beneath mountain walls and a waxing moon, swiftly and silently like falling snow they were stalking . . . ambushing right along the top of the ridgeline on the other side.

"They might have smelt the food we cooked or they might have smelt human flesh. They must be starving . . . needed meat . . . may be food was hard to come by for them in this frozen abode" my paralyzed brain knocked.

Chime and I were shivering out of fear; the muscle in my body did the clench thing. We cornered ourselves . . . Chime clutched me tightly; her nails penetrated into my left hand skin.

In the chilling weather, seeing those leopards Father's forehead glistened with perspiration. He crawled inside the cave, pushing us inside as much as he could. Buzzed with adrenaline I stood, thinking of the entire spine-tingling close encounter, I couldn't imagine going toe-to-toe with them.

We slammed against wall behind a huge stone; we sat, motionless and completely silent, watching the snow leopards.

They passed over snow, scree and boulders.

Peering through the dark night I watched them.

The snow leopards moved rippling silently down a gully of rocks; padding straight up to us they slung around the other side of the river. The black objects became clearer and darker; they were fully-grown and wailing their long, thick tails.

We didn't have hunting knife . . . rifle . . . Father was not at all prepared for this. No one in Zanskar carries such things during their journey on *Chadar*. 'They always say snow leopard doesn't attack human' but it was a myth . . . inevitability happened.

The sighting of grey shapes devastated me.

Absent minded, Father searched for some weapon . . . anything that would help him defend us. Then he picked up his stick from the bedside; removed knife from his bag, and tied the knife with the stick . . . his hands were trembling, out of fear he dropped it twice.

"Stay behind me and close your eyes." He murmured, panting, making stealthy swoops with his hand.

Terror seized us all. Holding his stick with two hands Father was ready to attack them. "What this little knife would do in front of those predators?" I wondered.

They were grunting intensely . . . chuffing . . . as if communicating with each other 'Who would leap upon us?' Any moment they could attack us.

"What if they eat Father first? Then I will be left alone with Chime . . . how I will fight with them?" daunting thoughts poured into my mind. I imagined "My head in his mouth . . . and I am touching his taste buds. His claw under my neck . . . pulling, chewing, ripping . . ."

Chime was sobbing; I sealed her mouth with my hand . . . my arm around her neck. Huddled in one corner, together we waited for our death to arrive . . .

Those vertical pupils locked on to us; they were intently staring at us . . . no doubt we caught their attention. I couldn't count how many snow leopards were there . . . but certainly more than two.

They were taking their own time to attack, as if they knew we could not run anywhere else; tension rose. Rescue, that hour was out of question.

I wondered, "Where is Goddess Mother Earth? Why she is not helping us? Why she is not taking those creatures underground? People always talk about God, where is He? What wrong we did that we are facing such a horrifying vulnerable condition?"

My inherent desire was to flee . . . but where?

I suddenly remembered there was another unexposed area in the cave. "It may lead us somewhere" I assumed. Gathering leftover courage I decided to move towards the other part of the cave; I hoped it would lead us to some safer place. Creepily, beyond the ineffectual glare of our fire, I crawled towards that area . . . it was getting darker with my every step. I bent to my left . . . after four-five steps there was a bend to my right . . . One bat flew over brushing my head. I hurt my knees while crawling. I approached the area and I ran into stonewall.

Death was certain. We were going to be eaten by a living nightmare.

I crawled back to Chime. Father had stood still as if statue. With every passing second death was teasing us. We were in dilemma. "Why are they not attacking us?"

Where nature was still considered the abode of the spirits and all animals were divine; amid lore rich in reverence for all living things, the snow leopard continued to menace.

Beneath mountain walls and a waxing moon, the most powerful, agile cats were howling . . . Their howling sound was a mixture between a cat and a wolf . . .

Time passed at a snail's speed, they still didn't attack. Tension was building by every second.

One of them walked upslope to a rocky cliff swaying his head back slightly and sat quietly, all the time carefully watching his kill. In the distance, other laid prone just behind the ridgeline . . . leaving their heads visible, making very little motion . . . locating a moving sidewalk.

Clearly, snow leopards were not about to share their dinner with each other.

We heard a low moaning cry echoing through the valley.

We heard the call several more times; they were still there.

Landscape stood completely still.

After resting on top of the cliff for a few minutes, the snow leopard came back towards us, descending just a little down; he finally made his decision to leap upon us and the others followed him; slipping like ghosts through the snow and boulder fields.

We heard different noises . . . hissing, cracking, as if someone is walking on broken crockery . . . collapsing of rocks . . . thud of their long and powerful hind limbs . . . The cracking and popping sounds spread in the valley; it was nerve racking.

Fear ripped into my lungs, robbing me off all oxygen. I heard my own pulses; my heart palpitated with chilling fear that was setting in. Only God could save us.

Our life cracked with each sound.

To invoke the good spirits in the valley, Father murmured '*Om Mani Padme Hum . . . Om Mani Padme Hum . . .*' Chime too, uttered, '*Om Mani . . . Om Mani . . .*'

Our destiny was playing hide and sick with us. I did not understand what it was offering us.

"Death or Life?"

At one point, their noise dwindled into the gloom. It seemed they vanished beyond canyons.

The grey, cold morning was utterly quiet, the silence broken only by the occasional call of a bird.

The fire of dawn lighted the path.

Father, cautiously moved towards the entrance squirming, scanned the area.

Father had drained his energy; dropping the knife he sat on the floor, breathing rapidly. We both were in his arms . . . half alive, half dead. Father muttered nervously, "I didn't see them, but that doesn't mean they have left. They could be around. We will leave once it becomes bright. Let's pack our luggage and be ready."

We were silent; it was probably a self-realization phase. This journey could turn an ill fated journey; a fatal blow. We were going to bleed to death.

In a remarkable piece of good fortune, we were alive.

The first light of the day picked its way through the haze into the cavern; we felt secure. May be some good spirits in the cave protected us, may be Goddess Mother Earth blessed us.

I couldn't understand when the food was so close, then 'WHY'? 'Why didn't they kill us?'

There were many questions . . . many why . . . might be 'snow leopards don't attack humans' was not a myth . . . with too many unknown reasoning's I wished to escape from the cave at the earliest.

7

TREE OF LIFE

The frozen valley was shimmering under the sun like thousands of diamonds.

We were at the cave entrance . . . before we would walk out I looked back; I bid a goodbye to this life savior cave. I prayed, "God, let there not be snow leopards outside; help us to reach the school on time. Guard us from evil spirits."

Loaded with our bags, we followed Father with new spirit. With stealthy silent steps, Father advanced further, scanning the vicinity acutely. His knife still attached to the stick like a soldier's rifle; pointing outwards.

Chime and I were a couple of feet away from Father, hesitant to move ahead, waiting for his signal for safety. Chime whispered, "Will they be still outside, brother?"

"I hope they are not," I muttered.

Father's grip on the knife tightened; Chime slid behind me.

There was no sign of leopards . . . no miffs . . . no growls; he was relieved. Inhaling fresh air briefly, he said, "Kids, let's go, we are safe now." Chime, glued to the floor, asked frantically "Are you sure Father, they are not there?"

Previous night's trauma obsessed her. "Okay, I move ahead and you follow me" Father said convincingly. He lifted his feet to move ahead . . . thud . . .

Thunderous sound echoed in the cave . . .

Ice beneath Father's feet cracked . . . *Chadar* swallowed him. The sound of rushing river filled my ears. We both ran towards him, a large patch of ice had thawed pitching Father into the icy water. He tumbled all the way down. The ice along the river's edge cracked with the impact. Father had shattered underneath the thin ice shelf.

The deep, penetrating cold shocked my senses; raw fear devoured me, leaving me riveted to the spot.

'Father . . . .' Our voices rose through the valley softly . . . then horrible screams filled the air.

We were crying out loud. It was sheer panic. No time to think, to react, it just happened quickly.

He went off the edge and disappeared. A rip current swept him. He was struggling to orient himself and get air in frenzy. Helplessly, we were watching Father battling with the strong current beneath the ice.

His entire body submerged. Water was a barrier between air and his lungs . . . he was waving his arms and legs frantically. "Has he drowned?" I thought. He struggled to keep his head above water and every time he would come back up for the air; another wave would crash down on top of him. The cold water was hitting his face so hard that he could neither open his eyes nor his mouth to breathe. Each second in freezing water was a fight for survival.

My sight became blurred than ever, head began to spin and my body became so numb I couldn't even feel my own existence any more. "Is he dead?" I talked to myself in my head, as if in a mental prison.

I remember black and red rings, the only thing I could see . . .

Minutes went by, I was still crying. The air was expelled creating bubbles, Father was running out of breath; every passing bit ceased Father's life.

I looked up to the sky and prayed . . . nothing left in me, absolutely nothing . . . I thought about Maa . . . this whole world . . .

He was flapping the arms to either side with a slanted body position just above the surface. He tried to angle his feet downstream to avoid hitting any obstacles with his head . . . Any blunt trauma to the head could knock him out . . . he was being enveloped in a massive weight; his arms and legs were just not strong enough.

He was struggling for a long stretch of time . . . rescue was elicited.

We were panicking . . . screaming . . .

Water level varied, he tried to grab reeds to pull himself out in vain. The river was competing with the speed of light; waves were crashing into cliffs, sculpting new curves. The current carried Father some miles away . . . And then he rammed into big icy rock, bounced back . . . scraped and bruised he started bleeding. Blue water merged with red.

Feelings detached; I heard a roaring in my ears.

The moment he hit the rock, strap of his shoulder bag entangled with a protruding icy ledge; the cheese container strap loosen by the pressure of the water. The next moment it was all open . . . one by one all cheese blocks started floating on the waves. The empty cheese container was tumbling . . . .

Father tried hard to get rid off his shoulder bag to grab the floating cheese blocks . . . he was trying to recapture vanished cheese blocks; they drifted away . . . far beyond his sight.

We could see his head bobbing in the water, for a while Father was out of sight . . .

He came up at last, but only for a few brief seconds . . . I was feeling dizzy, everything went yellow; there was no sound . . . no sensation at all. I felt a lump in my throat. He was choking on the bubbles.

Since his bag's strap had hooked up he couldn't move, in the struggle the bag torn. He then released the bag, fighting to keep from sinking, gasping at the pain of the intense cold. He then tried to hold the rock on the bank of the river; but it sent him further deep in the water. He was now fighting for his life. The waves tossed him; he lost his sense of direction. And then suddenly he bounced back on the rock, this time he managed to hold the rock. Exhausted he holding the rock started breathing heavily.

Chime was whining. I was screaming, "Father, please come back . . . please Father . . . please."

He saw us weeping. Looking at our yelling faces, he plunged in with the very last ounce of his effort, grappling with river with sloppy strokes he was moving towards us. We were nothing but his final destination; he was thrashing his arms and legs in an attempt to tread water; next moment he touched us. Apart from the most traumatic stress, we gave him hand. I had no strength left. We were struggling to pull his cold, heavy body and tried to hold on him, this had an effect of pulling us down. I grabbed his neck, he rested his elbows on the floor; his head in the air. Chime bent down to hold his arm and when she did, the coral in her pocket fell into the water; a good luck charm uncle Tsering once given was no more with us. Tumbling down from her pocket it immersed in the ferocious river.

He emerged from the river; his lungs were bursting with the need for breath when he finally found the air. Crawling towards the cave, he lay on the floor. He drenched in the frigid water for what seemed an eternity. Icy water had entered his bloodstream sucking a lot from him. He was paler than white and breathing was extremely hard.

He was shaking uncontrollably; he couldn't cope with the cold. His wet clothes were rapidly stealing heat from his body.

Father was stuck in a dazed state for a while afterwards. Chime sat by his side; waiting for him to open the eyes. Convulsive sobs racked her body. Her throat was parched from all that blubber.

I wished if uncle Tsering would have been around; he would have helped us. There was a very sudden, very overwhelming sense of panic; paralyzed with fear I couldn't command my hands to move; I had to wake him up. Wasting each moment meant losing at life; Father was out of water but not safe. He had subsided not just into a river but Zanskar River. Hastily, I removed his wet clothes, shoes and gloves. Chime removed his socks. I then wrapped his body with a blanket.

Father was half dead; I tried to push him inside the sleeping bag with all my strength. It was not enough to keep Father warm; we needed a fire.

Swallowing water made him nauseous, inhaling made breathing difficult. Nature had shown another color, but this time not to please us.

I started looking for matchstick to light the fire; I remembered Father had kept it in his right side pocket of *goncha*. I reached his *goncha* for matchsticks, they were dripping wet. I soaked them with my sweater to dry; then scrubbed the matchsticks one by one in vain; they had caught moisture, none of them worked. My hopes fizzled along with the moist sticks.

Fortunately last night's lit fire was still sputtering. I started blowing it; observing a red glow I placed tinder on top of the embers. With my running nose I was blowing the fire gently to influence fresh air on the hot spot, I felt dizzy and my eyes started burning. I faced hard time lighting the fire. After adding more wood, it burst into flames.

Terrified, Chime was still crying. "Father please, get up . . ." she kept saying constantly. Father was still unconscious. I started rubbing his feet and asked Chime to rub his palms to keep him warm.

While rubbing his feet I noticed wound; his feet was bleeding. I collected an ash from the previous night's burnt out wood and smudged it into the wound to stop the bleeding.

An hour passed . . . we were nervous; His body was cold and showed no signs of life.

Unscathed after lengthy submersion in very cold water, he opened his eyes . . . waves of relief rippled down my spin. We both hugged him. He was saved from the ordeal!

The blood drained from his face. He struggled to get up; covering himself with the blanket he hunkered down beside the stone, staring apprehensively into infinite.

Tears streamed down his cheeks.

"My goodwill earned in the market flown away . . . it took all my life to earn and minutes to lose . . . what they will think of me? I am a thief? Who didn't turn back after receiving the payments? How we are going to spend our next ten months without grocery? That was my whole year's savings . . ." He was talking to himself; his gaze fixed at the river for long . . . surveying the extent of disaster, his face distorted.

"Where is God? Where are those spirits? Where is *Sharshok* who saves everyone on this journey?" An angry frown creased his forehead. He mistrusted the future; it was traitorous.

"All my savings have gone. I don't know how I will submit your school fees?" he murmured.

"Why he is talking to himself?" I asked myself. A haze of fear surrounded me. He fell on his knees, clutching his head in despair he mourned, "May be, I am reaping what I have sown; I am wiping off my past debts now."

I gathered my thoughts; wiping off his tears I said, "Father, once *Chadar* forms we will go back to our village." He didn't respond . . . his gaze fixed.

Father was wandering around in his own mind. I had to redeem him to bring into real world . . . world where we existed . . . world where Maa was waiting for him . . .

Looking into his eyes, I continued, "We have four yaks with us Father; Yoko's father has only one. They are still happy; then why can't we?" I was hoping he would answer; but he was at a loss of words.

Holding Father's numb hand, Chime whispered, "I am missing Maa and our yaks. I feel like going home, Father."

The cave was silent; Father was lifeless as if stone. He was neither seeing nor listening. "Is he frozen to death or the reality?" I pondered.

Pale sunlight dappled the cave. In a low gravelly voice, he uttered, "*Chadar* has melted untimely . . . in a day or two, whenever it forms we will go back."

We huddled together and stared apprehensively into the emptiness. Time stood still for us. True . . . Sun was blazing in the sky; reflecting the path, but there was still darkness . . . darkness in my mind . . . we had lost our path; our faith in good spirits . . .

"Why didn't we stay back with uncle Tsering? Why Father was in a hurry? If we had waited; we wouldn't have faced the leopards; Father wouldn't have fallen into the river and lost his cheese" my subconscious kept saying. I wished if I could reverse the wheel of *'Kalachakra'*—the Wheel of Time . . . I wanted to go back to uncle Tsering and start the journey with them safely.

I felt sad for Chime; Destiny didn't allow her to make it till school.

She curled up near Father calmly, toying with her yellow ribbon. May be she realized her secure world was around Father; there was nothing more substantial than Father's presence, and that she was again in safe hands.

Evening crashed into the ground. Breaking the prolonged silence Chime said, "Father I am hungry." Father was not responsive. Wearily, I reached my sack to get the Tiffin. Some breads—*'balep korkun'* remained. Luckily Maa had packed them in my bag. Every year for me, she used to pack these homemade flat breads; round and thin. This time she packed them for Chime too. The packets of *skiu* had already washed out with Father's luggage. I picked up bread, breaking it into half I gave it to Chime.

"Brother, aren't you hungry?" she questioned, munching the bread.

"No," I uttered. The resentful incident had eaten my appetite. I looked at Father; he had crouched in the corner, his mind poured with several thoughts. He pulled himself up to stand against the cave wall; as he stretched his hand, pain excruciated. His back muscle hurt when he hit the rock under water, his muscle almost torn apart when he stretched his hand. He was in a miserable state; just an attempt to stand made him collapse.

Neglecting the physical pain, Father picked up coal from the burnt out ashes and started darkening the thin dwindled grey outlines existed on one of the walls.

In such agony when he couldn't even stand properly, all his amassed reserves flown away; he was now smudging the coal on the wall, inking his hidden thoughts; portraying something. I couldn't read his mind. "Is he haunted? Or has he lost sanity?" my mind scared me. Awestruck, I was looking at him. Horrified Chime stood speechless by Father's weird behavior.

He was about to finish sketching; I recognized the image. The same tree; tree we always found in the monastery, a tree of refuge; a place of safety. Its branches blew in the winds of the void. *'Bodhi Tree'*—Tree of Life.

"Who depicted this Tree in this mysteriously hidden cave?" I asked myself.

"Could be Gods or spirits. Or may be passer-by monk rested here depicted this tree for meditation." Reel of possibilities ran in my mind.

In monastery, Lama had once told me beneath the similarly figured *Bodhi* Tree—the Great Tree of Enlightenment, *Buddha* redeemed the whole universe under its protective branches. *Buddha* transformed all negative temptations and energies and achieved perfect enlightenment under the same tree.

I wondered, "How his eyes noticed the slender lines of the trunk?" That was the only part devoid of algae.

Ancient Tibetan texts, thousands of hand-inked folios with beautiful illuminations and small paintings adorned the walls of crumbling cave. Indeed the divinities resided there.

The valuable artwork was ruined; someone raided the cave; or might be the religious pilgrims damaged the walls to collect souvenirs. Longer I spent time looking it revealed more . . . The cave was a storehouse of cultural wisdom.

Bowing against *Bodhi* Tree he said, "Thank you Lord. I don't have words to thank you, but I have a faith in you. I am an illiterate man, but I am sure about one thing, my fate has not cheated me of everything. You saved me not once but twice . . ."

He stared at the wall. I wondered what that Tree of Life had to do with his survival.

He then turned to us and said, "Last night leopards could kill us, but *Chadar* melted and they couldn't reach us. I saw death in their twinkling eyes. Any moment could kill us but it was something . . . the superior divine forces changed *Chadar* into a daunting river. I drowned and had almost surrendered to death. But something kept me moving; something that drew me towards you. I don't know how I gain the strength to push myself again the current but I tried till my last breath and reached you."

I was listening to his each word carefully; thinking about that Divine Superintendent. Chime was quiet.

'We are neither absolutely the servants nor the masters of our Karma.'

It seemed he gained his confidence back.

The sun had lost its brightness . . . pale moon had risen.

The fire was still burning. What we had lost was just a year of my studies and Father's one-year earnings; but had gained life in return. I was sure with hard work we could cope with it, but I couldn't imagine our life without Father; a man who mattered more to me than anything in the world.

'God does have a plan for every single person, even if it takes a while to see what it is. Knowing the purpose of life seems like an elusive undertaking.'

Haunting tones drifted over the mountains. Thanking God we went to bed.

My subconscious rejected wildness and undigested shadow side of nature; Tree of Life shadowed my mind.

8

FRAGILE SEED

*A*coppery sun had skimmed the horizon of Zanskar. The air was warm and steamy.

In the warehouse Maa was churning butter, in the barrel-shape wooden churn with broomstick handle . . . a long standing tradition, arduous and time-consuming . . . lading the sour cream into skimmed milk . . . minutes and hours of churning until she heard yaks grunting outside; their grunt made her distinctly uneasy.

She went to the verandah worriedly, to see why were they making so much noise . . . but couldn't find the cause.

From somewhere in the distance she saw few porters approaching . . . Her breathing shallowed.

Maa could see Uncle Yeshe, walking promptly towards her. He was a respected elderly man in our village; his lined face could speak of a hard life of labor.

Uncle Yeshe arrived with few other porters of the village. She was afraid that they had got some terrible news for her. Her face suddenly darkened.

Uncle Yeshe reached our home; he appeared calm and controlled. Choosing his words carefully, with a low, gravelly voice uncle Yeshe said, "Zampa, *Chadar* melted last night untimely."

Maa swallowed. Her tears stifled; she tried to read uncle Yeshe's mind.

He paused for a while and then continued, "This is the nature of *Chadar* to keep changing . . . to test our faith in her . . . our faith in our valleys."

All he could do was give my mother moral support. Aggregating his thoughts he continued, "We will pray for Norbu and children . . . Don't worry Zampa, if it has melted untimely, then it may also form."

Dachen, son of uncle Yeshe, a wiry, energetic man interrupted, "Father, Why are you giving false hopes to her? Everyone knows it is impossible to cross *Chadar* before six-seven days. Norbu has left with children two days back . . . people always drown into the chilling river if *Chadar* melts."

Maa was caught in the turmoil of her own thoughts, tears rolled down onto her cheeks.

Uncle Yeshe said, "Dachen, You better be quiet or leave from here . . . We had come here to give Zampa news about *Chadar* . . . not to discourage her. Haven't you ever seen before *Chadar* melting untimely and forming again the very next day?"

Uncle continued, "Zampa, *Chadar* has melted late in the night . . . Norbu must have refuge by then . . . he is an experienced man, he has crossed *Chadar* many times. I am sure though they are stuck, they must have sheltered at some safe place." Other porters agreed with uncle.

Dachen said, "I just hope whatever you are saying comes true, but these are just assumptions."

Ignoring Dachen uncle Yeshe said, "Zampa, don't listen to him. *Chadar* will definitely form soon . . . may be in a day or two . . . everything will be alright."

Listening to the news mother rushed inside the room. She collapsed on the floor. Uncle Lobsang and Aunt Nyima had arrived our house listening to the news. Uncle Lobsang sat with the other porters outside the room, on the verandah, Aunt Nyima was with my mother inside the room.

Maa could hear porters arguing outside the house. Yaks were still grunting.

One porter said, "Don't be so blunt Dachen. We came here to give her strength. Norbu is a nice man; he has never hurt anyone. We should wish for him and his children's safety. May the good spirits in the valley guide him."

Dachen replied, "Even if they are alive somewhere, they haven't taken supplies with them for a whole year. What if *Chadar* doesn't form for the entire year? And if they have refuge can they live without food and other resources for a year? Even if they are alive they might starve to death."

An argument between Dachen and other porters heated up.

Maa's mind entirely engulfed by deep fear; all she could do was just pray . . . pray for our safety . . . pray for our arrival. Aunt Nyima that night stayed with Maa.

All the assumptions were nothing but a fragile seed.

9

A Harsh Awakening

I succumbed to wakefulness. Sunshine poured through flooding the cave.

Cave submerged with river mellifluously . . . Father sat by the riverside, against the orange sky . . . still as stone . . . as if reading her; judging her depth or maybe pleading her to transform into ice so we could set ourselves for the home.

I walked up to him. The sun was warming . . . the snow was settling. Stealthy silent had stepped in; the roaring turquoise river tumbled through the valley.

Father said, "*Chadar* didn't form last night as well. We might have to stay here for another . . . he paused . . . and said, Might be for a week . . ."

Gazing at me with pensive eyes he continued, "By now your mother might have received the news about *Chadar*. She will be worried. I had promised her I would take care of you two; I assured her I would return soon with all year's staples."

He was speaking more like a friend than a father.

"We don't have enough food stock with us. We must consume it carefully now onwards. You are a grown up boy, Kaba; you can understand. But Chime? She is a little girl . . . she has dreams of going to school and seeing a new world . . . I have been reading them . . . and I can't see her dreams shatter . . . we have to deal with her carefully."

I tried to understand him; it was a harsh awakening.

Chime was still in the bed; I looked back at her. I wondered how long she had been sleeping. She blinked, shut her eyes and yawned. She blinked again trying to open her eyes.

The first thing she did was she moved to the corner where her tiny friends were lumped together.

"Ohh, you have already started working?" she inquired.

"Today we are going back to our village." Confidently, she told her friends. Her face erupting in a luminous smile as she addressed her new amigos, "I am going to meet Maa and my yaks . . . You know we have four yaks with us. Have you ever seen yaks?"

"No?" she answered on their behalf.

"Don't be fooled by their size . . . they are very polite. They are our cattle cousins and eat about a third of what we eat. The biggest one is Diki, very fat. Gesturing with hands she was explaining.

She's especially fond of treats, and thinks she should have them all. She is as black as coal, including her nose."

Showing her worn socks she said, "My Maa knitted these mixing Pema's and Rinzen's fur . . . grey and brown . . . Pema is second and Rinzen is number three. Compared to Diki, Rinzen and Pema are more humble and just a touch on their nose pleases them! Our Tashi has a crooked horn; she is least interested in being petted. She is the youngest of all."

"I always feed them range cakes," she spoke.

Chime was engaged in fascinating conversations.

She went on talking. "I will meet you during my next year's trip while going to school. I will ask Father to stay here, so I will get to see you," she blabbered.

Watching Chime and her friends I gathered all my thoughts and said, "You can spend some more time with them Chime. *Chadar* is not yet frozen."

My answer disappointed her. "Brother, when will it form? She asked.

"Whenever God will send snow," I replied.

"And when will He send the snow?" She inquired anxiously.

"Soon . . ." that's what I could say. I looked at Father; he looked at me for a long moment. "He would not have been so worried if we weren't both there with him," I thought.

To divert her attention, I said, "Let's fix up some breakfast for your friends."

I climbed on the rock to reach the ceiling and scrubbed algae with sharp stone; I gave algae to Chime. We both started feeding mossy food to her friends.

Father sorted the wood he had gathered; wood was not sufficient. It could hardly last for few couple of hours. Opening our bags he removed the Tiffin; food in the Tiffin could serve barely five days. A packet of *skiu* and some snacks Maa had given were left. But to cook *skiu* we needed fire. We had already lost our lantern in the river the other day.

Father gave us some snacks to eat and he himself ate very little. He drank the water we had already filled our bottles with . . . that too, carefully, sip by sip. We couldn't drink water straight from the river. He filled the empty bottles with river water and placed it underneath the ash to warm.

He then emptied matchbox and placed all sticks on the rock to dry them thinking we might use them later.

Chime was still busy playing with the ants . . .

Every passing hour made me feel uneasy. "What if *Chadar* doesn't form tonight? How will we get home? How can we live here without food, without fire? In the darkness . . . a world cut off from outside . . ." A haze of fear surrounded me.

It started getting colder; the sky deepened to dark blue. Father was still avoiding burning wood for fire to save them.

When it was coal dark and wind was unbearable, he lit the fire with leftover wood. We huddled around the fire. Father then got some ice to melt it.

I opened sleeping bags; before going to bed I prayed . . . asking God to form the *Chadar* so we could go home safely. I asked for the courage to undertake the current situation and the perseverance to continue to do it and the strength to complete it.

I thought of Maa; I missed her terribly.

Seeing me praying, Chime asked, "What are you praying brother?"

I said, "I am asking God to send snow so we can leave for home tomorrow." She too started praying with me . . . she snuggled in her sleeping bag. I lay down; wishing *Chadar* would freeze.

People always said in the village, miracles happen. And I had faith in it. I knew Miracle would happen . . . and *Chadar* would form.

They say, 'There are good spirits in the valleys. They take care of people; people who haven't done anything wrong to anyone, people who haven't hurt anyone.'

I had faith that those good spirits must be watching us from somewhere . . . and they would rescue us . . .

Chilly damp moonlight loomed overhead. I eventually drifted into an uneasy sleep.

Father was sleepless; he was trying to fuel the dyeing fire.

He added the left over piece of wood. Over and above, fire could not survive for more than an hour and it was a long night.

The Tree of Life was asking us to have Faith . . . The stars winked at us from a sky pitch black.

Dithering in the cold without fire we spent our last night.

That was the first night I slept without fire; it was tough. Chime was shivering more. She had painfully numb toes. Entire night, Father sat by her side wriggling her toes.

He had already given his blanket to her. All he had was his moist woolen *goncha*. Through the nights we struggled.

Midnight, Father checked the condition of the river. But it showed no sign of ice.

In the classroom, we always huddled around a small stove to protect ourselves from extreme cold weather; but we were neither in the school nor at home.

It was the coldest night of my life.

We were waiting for the first rays of the sun to penetrate in the cave so we would get some warmth. It was getting formidable with every passing hour.

Icy, dust-laden winds were blowing all the time. We couldn't withstand such dominating cold.

As the rays of sunlight poured through the cave we sat at the entrance to soak the sun . . . Father filled our bottles with water and buried under the ashes to add warmth into.

Warmth that caused Life to grow overcoming Death-giving cold . . .

IO

REALIZING EMPTINESS

Night faded into eternal darkness; darkness that dappled my mother's mind. Time stood still . . . Aunt Nyima counteracted mother's aloneness by simply being there. She was trying to reach out her pain; ease her burden . . .

"Zampa, *Chadar* melted last night untimely." Uncle Yeshe's words haunted her. "I must go to the banks," she murmured.

"Do you want to go to the bank this hour?" Nyima aunt asked.

"Yes . . . I want to see if *Chadar* is really melted or not; I don't believe in uncle Yeshe's words." She replied, anxiously.

"It is too late Zampa, with the first ray of the sun we will set for the river. I am sure, even if *Chadar* is melted, it will form overnight." Nyima aunt tried to convince Maa.

"I am sure, they will be safe. They must have sheltered somewhere safely." Maa consoled herself.

Frightening thoughts raced through her mind. The very moment she wanted to reach us; she wanted to see us in flesh and blood. But deep down, she knew the nature of *Chadar*. Possessed with unwelcomed thoughts she stayed up all night; without blinking an eye, counting her each breath, hoping for our safety.

"Gather yourself Zampa; don't lose hope . . ." Aunt Nyima said.

But that time she was just a loving mother and a loyal wife; who had given her entire life for the family. Her world surrounded by us.

Long before dawn, expectantly uncle Lobsang reached our home; Maa, along with Nyima aunty had been waiting for him. They hurried down wide, silent valley; through the towering whitened crags and gorges; as though driven by shuddering fear. The valley was filled with clouds. Lifting herself up onto the ice she walked with a heavy heart; with her every step her fear became heavier. Chasing the cold wind they reached the banks of the Zanskar River. As they made their way to the banks, dark, storm clouds built up in the sky; threatening to engulf at any moment.

A ghastly whiteness spread over her face. Her eyes didn't witness what her heart expected.

The only winter road in the remote enclave was melted; the region was once again inaccessible. The icy path we ventured three days back was vanished; leaving traces of blue, wavy ribbons behind. *Chadar* was melted.

Uncle Yeshe along with his fellow porters, were already on the banks. Maa was not the only one whose family had set their journey on *Chadar*; the villagers whose relatives had started their journey reached the banks to examine *Chadar*. Everyone was confronted by nature's power; it was life-threatening reality. Uncle Yeshe tried to calm them and stabilize the situation. It was indigestible side of *Chadar*.

"*Chadar* is always changing," someone said sadly. Someone wondered aloud "Who knows what condition the next day might hold?"

"A successful journey is just as much a matter of luck or maybe just a matter of time." There were quiet murmurs.

Maa was enveloped in unearthly silence; silence that muffled the sounds of whooshing river, the chatter of the people. She was suspended in a void.

The clouds still clung on to the mountains; raining could make the situation miserable. It was dramatic climate change villagers encountered.

Chadar was left with thin layers of ice with many cracks on it; each crack tore everyone's hope apart. Ice was floating on the thin layers; adamant to freeze. The intense fear fired through mother. "I need to see my Chime; she never walked on *Chadar* before. Mother Earth can't be so cruel," she cried and next moment collapsed on the ground as if *Chadar* cracked into pieces; her all hopes dissolved and melted away.

Aunt Nyima tried to empathize Maa; she was equally worried for us. "My heart is saying Zampa, they are safe in the valley somewhere; we will pray for them, they will return soon. Have faith," comforting Maa she said.

Uncle Yeshe uttered solemnly, "*Chadar* will form soon. This is not the month for her to freeze; she must wait. She can't deceive those who decided to walk on her with trust. She must form for Mother Nature's sake. Norbu will return with children, Zampa. And still they don't return then we will set our journey to find them. I am sure they haven't gone too long; they must not even have reached midway. Zampa, you are not alone. I am there with you. Don't forget Survival here is paramount."

Maa lost her sanity.

She sat on the banks for hours, lifeless; waiting to see *Chadar* form. It was not the game of magic wand; but the game of ferocious nature. It was time to show how daunting it can become.

A vast open nothingness had swallowed night; winter winds stung with icy slaps in the face.

However uncle Lobsang and Nyima aunty stayed with Maa. Nyima aunty requested Maa, "Let's go home Zampa. It's too late; your yaks must be hungry. You haven't fed them today. They need to be milked. Chime will be really upset with you, if she will learn that you didn't take care of them. What would Kaba's father think? Try to understand . . . they are your responsibility."

Aunt solaced her saying, "I promise you; we will come tomorrow again in the morning. Be strong and take care of yaks for Chime's sake, they are not just cattle but part of your family. Kaba's father has looked after them all these years as his children. You can't abandon them."

It was one of the most devastating days for Maa. Her world was collapsed but she was not the one left behind; our yaks were alone too. Our family couldn't be completed without their presence. They couldn't speak; but had sensed the inevitable long before any human being could. Maa then realized reason behind their grunting; it was an evidence of strong emotional bonding.

'Realizing the emptiness of self: Zankari woman lives her life struggling; as men in the family always have to cross the deadly *Chadar* to feed the family, their children as well have to leave home to join the school for their better future.'

My mother experienced the self-emptiness that day . . . no woman in Zanskar wants to think off.

'They say: Emptiness is a mode of perception, a way of looking at experience. It adds nothing to, and takes nothing away. You look at the events in the mind and the senses with no thoughts of whether there is anything lying behind them.'

11

THE BURIED THOUGHTS

No leaf drifted; nor wind blew; the sky was silent. Gloomy days froze into a void. Goddess Mother Earth didn't show mercy.

Cracking frostiness of the moist air sun entered our cave daily, for half an hour; we bathed into the warmness every day as if ritual. Those few moments energized us.

Whole day we sat inside the cave as if Mother Earth punished us and warned us not to move out of the cave. "But what is my mistake? Why Mother Earth is punishing me? Not only me also my dearest Chime and Father too?" I suspected. Uncle Tsering's word echoed in my mind "We should cherish her . . . instead we are destroying her . . . the warming temperature is a result of our spiritual failings. We have become too materialistic . . ."

"What does it mean we are destroying her? What is spiritual failing?" My curious, childlike mind asked me. I decided to ask uncle Tsering what he really meant when he said we are destroying our Mother Earth.

"But where uncle Tsering will be?" a concerning thought erupted in my mind.

Every night we went to the bed after prayers; asking GOD to stitch the blanket of ice overnight.

God was silent; anxiously we waited for his answer; he never spoke. We were furious, because our paths had led us away from mother and home. None of our prayer had been accepted; things kept on worsening.

We spent every night hoping morning will show us our way to home but adamant *Chadar* disappointed us each morning.

For hours, crouched in one corner I wondered, "What did God think when he created this entity? What made him paint the trees green and water blue? Why can't water be green? Why snow is white? Why the sky changes its color. Why can't it be static . . . only pale blue; it seems, like the human sky too has mood swings? He changed into orange when furious; yellow when happy and purple when meditating . . ."

I stared at canyons to learn their grandness; humungous they were! I wished if I could conquer them. I imagined myself standing atop the cliff, to find if there is any other route that would take us home. I wanted to be the nature: may be the leaf; so I could fly along with the singing wind and reach my Maa. Or may be the river; so I could flow towards our village; may the butterfly Chime always played with. But I had no magic wand to wave.

The abode we were living into was too real; rather awaking.

Home . . . I realized such a safe place! Nothing on this planet could be secured than mother's arms. I missed her terribly. I missed the way she woke me up every morning and I cribbed; I missed her *po-cha*; I missed to seeing weaving my fur coat; I wanted to feel the soft, warm coat. I missed the kindness, love reflected in her dark, black eyes. I didn't know whether this place would become our home for long.

I wished if I could talk to the river once and request her to freeze so I can go and see Maa.

My heart cried out "Don't lose hope."

But nature locked away the secrets. We were battling our inner selves, against the emptiness, against the darkness.

Beneath frigid dawn, Father sat at the edge of the cave silently, staring at his own distorted reflection in the river; his tired eyes gazing at the lost path.

Time cracked the firm ice; the shiny, white pieces floated on to the river, drifted away as they never belonged to each other. What's left behind was just cold, blue water; so cold that my mind became numb, my thoughts frosted.

My presence shadowed Father. I had no courage to ask him anything; nor did he have any answers.

I could hear the rocks grinding together on the riverbed.

Glaciers melted into the river. Its every drop buried my thoughts; our opportunity to get out of the cave evaporated under the scalding sun, our luck was tossed up.

Chime spent most of her time talking to her pets: Workaholic ants; she fetched food for them, fed them, and observed them eating; observed them loading the grains on their tiny shoulders. Those smart ants hid their staple somewhere deep inside the rocky walls and always crawled back to grab some more. They were busier than anyone else on this planet. Chime named the ant 'Queen Nima.'

Few more insects made friends with her. She introduced them to me. Everyone had unique name but all I can remember is yellow, green, red, brown abstract shapes . . . buzzing, humming, crawling, and flying around. For me they were just creatures; creation of God; and he is the one who knows the purpose behind creating them. But for her they were nothing but friends. Her enigma dragged every tiny, living creature; whoever was living in that empty space, on this land. That was her land: 'Chime Land.' She lived in that fantasy world.

I realized the great task in life is to find reality. This cave, every stone in the cave, the sand, every tree on the banks, every leaf on the tree, the sky; the snow; everything was real; and for the matter of fact melted *Chadar* was real too.

'Reality is not something that we can encounter through logic or reason; Reality is something that makes us feel the Supreme Power.'

Mighty, superior forces played climatic game with us.

I understood the true power of cold during those days. It made our teeth clatter, our fingers and toes went numb and our bodies shivered. But that's not the worst of it. The true power of cold lied in the way it sapped our morale out of us. It dampened our spirits to its lowest, it made us doubt ourselves. Those were the nights, we all, faced the cold at its worst.

A week eloped with ice trail; crystal clear river rushed towards Ladakh, hurriedly. *Chadar* ditched us; we were assured that she would certainly not return to us for a year.

We were left with two days' snacks. We wanted to get out of the cave; it would be impossible to survive without any resources. Avoiding having a second portion of diet Father and I started eating once a day. We knew it would not be useful if we had to survive for long; we needed to find out some way . . .

12

GUARDIAN SPIRITS

It was the tenth day, *Chadar* was still adamant; ice showed no presence.

That was the day I realized what hunger really is. Our Tiffin was empty; Snacks, Maa had packed in our Tiffin lasted only for a week. Whatever Father carried hungry river ate it all; food was over.

Often when, I felt hungry at home, I could simply tell Maa; and she would always cook *thukpa* or spicy stew potatoes . . . my favorite. She loved to surprise me and Chime with milk curd pastry. After churning butter, Maa used to store the savior residue in a wooden container; and used it with barley flour to make those yummy pastries. That day would always turn into complete delight for us.

If nothing then we used to drink yak milk.

The place we were trapped was not our home; I couldn't dare to ask Father for food. I was aware there is nothing Father can do; there was no stored staple; no yak milk. I struggled hard to bear with my hunger.

It was early noon, Father, as usual had sat on the edge of the cave, helplessly. Chime withdrew herself from her alcove; quietly, scanning around she reached my sack. I realized she is definitely looking for Tiffin. She removed the Tiffin from my sack; clutching the Tiffin in both hands, with her delicate fingers she pulled the clasp to release its treasure; her eyes narrowed, face turned red. Finally, she managed to open it; its lid hung from the squeaking hinges on the side. The odor smacked my nose as she opened it. Her face turned into a stale flower when she found the Tiffin empty.

The disappointment on her face was pungent; she stood empty-handed catching a whiff.

She approached Father. "Father, I am feeling hungry, the Tiffin is empty. When will we go home?" she said in a gravely low voice.

Father embraced her in his arms, "Do you miss your Maa, Chime?" he asked. Chime nodded wearily.

He further said, "Whenever you are home, Maa takes care of you, right?"

Chime said, "Yes."

Pointing at the Tree of Life Father said, "Here, in this desolated space, this Tree is your mother. We are not alone; God will send our guardian spirits to take care of us. If the night is dark they are on our side, if we feel afraid we can pray and ask them to protect us. Isn't it wonderful to know, Chime? You pray for help, and good spirit of the valley will come to rescue us.

They see everything we do. They hear everything we say. They go every place with us. They are with us when we play. They are on our side when we eat. They stand at our bed when we sleep. They hear our prayer and protect us from evil, danger and sin. Since our good spirits are always at our side we must make them glad with everything we do."

He was speaking enchantingly; his every promising word lifted my spirit.

Chime questioned Father innocently, "Are the guardian spirits around Uncle Tsering and his group as well, Father?"

Father understood the depth of her question; he knew what exactly Chime meant. He was at a loss of words. To avert her mind he said, "Did you feed your friends today? You will upset our God if you won't feed them, and then he will not send our guardian spirits to help us."

Getting up from his seat, Father scrubbed the algae and gave it to her to feed the ants. He was sure he couldn't hold the situation for long; he had to find some food.

We were hungry, cold and tired. I could feel my stomach growling.

Father was sunken in dark thoughts; the sky was glowing. Suddenly he got up and started searching for something.

"But what is he looking for? What would he find in this barren cave; ancient stones?" my inner voice questioned me. For us finding treasure was easier than finding food.

He moved to the end of the corner, behind a huge stone and stood there staring at the stone. He seemed to be engaged in some kind of struggle and then he glanced up; a decision made.

I wondered, "This ancient stone must have lived for long in this cave; he must have witnessed many monks who refuge in the cave, chanted . . . meditated . . . and crafted enchanting scripts on the rocky walls."

It was not an ordinary stone; it looked like a huge sea turtle.

"But what Father is finding behind this stone?" my confused mind questioned.

He breathed heavily; dropping hands forward he touched the green, mossy stone with his long, thin hands. Before I could sense his action, he started rotating the stubborn stone cautiously from corner to corner. With every move, his veins palpitated. It looked like the large, lazy turtle finally decided to move first time from his place; it seemed walking slowly he was trying to reach the banks of the river to swim.

I stood clueless; it required strength to push the stone. I knew that I would hardly help him; I was nothing but a fragile crop then; a crop that any wind could easily blow away. Something in me asked to move forward to help Father and the next moment I was with him, helping him to move the stone.

That moment I wished badly if I would have been a grown up man. Thinking we are playing some game, Chime dashed towards us to give a helping hand.

Father yelled at me, "Kaba, you both stay away from the stone; or else you would hurt yourself." Unwillingly, I shifted aside and pulled Chime near me; standing in one corner I looked at Father helplessly. My heart was not ready to give up; but I didn't want Father to get mad at us. At each exertion sweat poured from his head and rest of his body . . . his knees were rubbing against the raw surface; his *goncha* muddied with algae and dirt.

He rested for a while gasping for breath. Gathering all his strength he started rolling the stone again; edges of it were chipping and scratching the ground. After an hour's struggle he managed to move the heavy stone towards the cave entrance. I yet didn't understand the reason behind pushing the stone towards the edge; all I could do was wait and watch. Picking up one small, sharp stone from the ground, Father scrubbed the huge stone to remove the algae from the surface; the layer was thick. He scrubbed the top; then all the side. When it was clean enough to stand Father climbed upon it. He stood on top of it leaning outwards, trying to reach the outer edges of the cave; struggling to climb up. His feet were making a lot of noise. Somehow he placed his right hand onto the top of the cave but it slipped due to layered algae and melted snow.

Putting most of his body weight on his feet, balancing himself on the stone, keeping the body motionless he started scrubbing at the algae with his right hand.

After few minutes' trial, he dropped his one knee down while the other knee was up in the air, swinging violently like a pendulum. Later finding his foothold, he placed the foot back on the stone to gain strength. It demanded more endurance; his hands burnt horribly with friction but he was feeling impatient with the delay. Seeing him traversing back and forth scared Chime and me. We didn't understand what Father was up to.

Attempting various routes, wiggling and resituating, slipping of the hold, loosing balance he finally gave up. He had pushed himself to limit but it required more strength; he had no stamina left. He was tired physically, not mentally.

He washed his face with cold, river water; tried to clean his stained *goncha*. He had one *goncha* left, he hadn't changed it in the past ten days; it was now torn on knees and elbows.

There was no fire, no food. Father had realized there was no escape; no way out. Waves of darkness rippled in our mind.

We filled our stomachs with water that day. Reciting *'Om Mani Padme Hum'* we went to bed.

We succeeded planting a leaf of 'Patience' to our Tree of Life that night.

I tossed and turned in my bed, woke up more than once, wondering where the guardian spirits had gone. I was expecting help from an angel . . . . some magic to happen. "Would we starve to death?" my impatient mind asked.

All I was thinking about miracles, magic, guardians, spirits, angels; trying to remember when I first time heard about them.

With eyes closed, I was viewing the Tree of Life in my dreams.

I sensed the tree exhausted a high, bright energy. I could see whirling clouds, dancing angels and beautifully wrinkled faces of old sages laughing in the tree bark. I walked over a brightly illuminated tree in the darkness of the cave and knelt beneath it. I said, "Father says, your presence is next to GOD. You listen to the prayers if we pray soulfully, then why are you not listening to me, to Chime? Why you aren't passing our prayers to Almighty? 'If you keep adverse forces and bad spirits away, then what is the supreme power that is transforming our conditions from bad to worse?"

Not able to sleep, waking up from the partial dream, I saw the moonlight falling inside the cave covering only the outlined sketch of the Tree of Life. The tree was glowing as if God had enlightened it.

Looking at it, I wondered, "Is this Tree of Life the first tree on the planet? Did God create tree first and then men? Was man alone when God sent him on the earth?" All probabilities littered my mind, and then I remembered a lesson I had learnt in school last year about life of pre-historic man.

'Prehistoric man', I wanted to share this exciting thought with Chime.

Clutching her stomach tight, with both hands she was snuggling in her sleeping bag . . . shifting from one corner to another constantly.

I called her, "Chime, are you up?"

She responded palely, "Yes brother, I can't sleep tonight. I am hungry?"

"Do you want to know how man appeared on the earth the very first time?"

"How?" she said.

"Hundreds of thousands of years ago men evolved from an apelike creature; something called hominoids. I don't know what that exactly means. And you know what? They used to live in caves. They had no easy access to food, shelter and clothing. They used to make clothes with animal skin."

"The way Maa makes with yak fur?" she asked.

"Yes, we wear them along with our *gonchas*; but these men and women used to simply wrap these skins around them." I answered.

"How silly!" She exclaimed.

I continued with my little knowledge, "They didn't know what home was then, they painted their caves and made it their home. For food they hunted animals like mammoths, bulls, wild beers."

"Who is mammoth?" She asked curiously.

"The mammoth was a large elephant—like animal with hairy skin. It had ridged teeth."

Father too was listening.

"What did they used to eat?" She came up with another query.

"Using the stones, wood, animal bones, their teeth these men made sharp weapons like spears, bow and arrow for hunting. There were no pulses, no rice, and no cheese then. They used to eat raw animals and plants for survival until they discovered fire."

I realized how important fire was when I explained it to her. We had been fighting against cold past ten days without fire . . .

I went on and on until I realized Chime had fallen asleep.

Towering cliffs and the raging river had sealed us off from the outer world.

13

CAVERNOUS HOME

11th day.
  I reclined in the darkness of cave. The previous night too, brought bitter coldness along with her.

Chime, curled up in her sleeping bag took turns in intervals.

I had attempted to fall asleep, but failed.

Time was passing at a snail's pace. Dawn came seeping down mountainsides . . . cold wind chased the warmth of the day.

Sluggishly, I got up tossing my sleeping bag. "Has *Chadar* formed?" The first thing popped in my mind. I sat in my bed for a few seconds; cold wind snapped my thought, I heard the sound of the laughing river; she was laughing at our helplessness. Ten days passed; we were still in the cave.

In the dim light of dawn, movement across the cave caught my attention; it was dark and shadowy. The fleeting but distinctly human shape passed quickly over the far end of the cave.

I rubbed knuckles into my eyes to drive away the sleep. When I observed the figure consciously, I realized it was Father; he was sweeping the cave.

Approaching him I asked, "Why are you sweeping Father?" His narrow eyes twinkled; he said enthusiastically, "Kaba, now this cave is our home for some time." His answer was firm and assuring.

"This cave is our home? What is he saying? Is this real or I am still dwelling over my last night's memories of cave and early man?" snapped my mind. I pinched myself to knock off the thought; I was awake and whatever Father said was real.

He continued worriedly, "I don't know when *Chadar* will form; it might be a week . . . might be a year, if we are unfortunate. God has given us a chance to survive; we should not suspect His doings."

He paused; thinking deeply he said, "He has chosen us . . . may be to test our faith in Him. Let's not disappoint Him. We should prepare ourselves and make this small place a little cleaner. I am cleaning this cave so we can feel homely here. We must welcome His every act; we must accept every day as it comes; without thinking about tomorrow." I nodded obediently.

Our murmurs woke Chime up. She was half awake, half asleep. Stretching herself, yawning, she sat in her bed; she looked pale. Her yellow ribbons loosened; her silky pigtails messed up.

"Did God send snow last night, Father?" She questioned anxiously, playing with her loose pigtail; trying to tie the ribbon. Father became speechless listening to Chime's question. Worry shadowed his face.

To break the silence I said, "No Chime, it didn't snow." My unwelcoming answer saddened her. I told her, "Chime, we are going to play a game?"

"What game, brother?" She asked with sleepy eyes, yawning.

"Now onwards, this cave is our home, Chime. God has offered us a chance to exist as a first human on this earth and we have to stay here till *Chadar* forms. We have to source our food and fire," I was more nervous than excited.

"Are we going to live like the pre-historic man you told us about last night? Are we going to dress like them?" Chime jumped with her queries. Father and I laughed at her question.

"No dear," Father answered.

"You have clothes with you which your mother had given. We can wash them here, so you can keep changing them. But I might have to dress like a caveman," he said, pointing at his own clothes.

Chime giggled; the shadow of smile crossed Father's lips.

He had used his *goncha* for ten days. He would wash whenever it muddied and wear it again.

River swept away his clothes along with his luggage.

His words offered a small glimmer of strength in an otherwise unbearable situation.

Never in my wildest dream I had imagined that he would consider my thoughts of caveman seriously . . . I had shared the idea of a caveman with Chime previous night vaguely without any purpose. My thoughts were random; may be to deprive myself from hunger I had kept talking that night. But the idea of living in a cave inspired Father; he was serious.

We both cleaned the cave as much as we could. Our cave was not brightly colored like our home; nor decorated. Floor was not mud washed but pebbled. It didn't bear ornately carved windows to let in sunlight neither the blue painted wooden door nor the verandah.

I missed our kitchen with a cozy stove; the space we always tied our Rinzin, Pema, Tashi and Dikki; the main living space, the soft, woolen rugs. I missed the warm and comfortable homely feeling.

I realized my ideal home had gone for some time now and I hoped I would return village home soon.

I realized we were not homeless; God had provided us a shelter.

I thought, "I must be grateful for God's kindness. If he had wished we could be, by now, underneath the freezing cold river; but we were safe and together."

Worry reflected through his thin eyes. "I know it will take a while for us to make this cave truly a home. But when we will do; this place will become lifetime memory."

"Let me see, if I can catch something from river to eat," withdrawing himself from conversation he said. He emptied my bag, kept all my belongings in one corner and stood on the verge of the river . . . studying the river.

I went to the river to wash my ragged pants, my already faded shirt.

Water was glowing as lit within.

The ice had melted away; a narrow strip of slippery ice remained . . . clinging to the mountain.

Winter lived high in the snow, entire summer watching from frosted heights, scheming for the beauty of the Himalayas.

Spreading the soaked clothes on the rock I went inside the cave. I wore another pair of clothes, the left over pair.

Chime was feeding algae to her friends as usual; she had seemed settled down in our new home.

I thought, "How lucky these ants are! They are filling their tiny stomach with algae." Every day she fed them with love and care, like my mother used to serve food to me, forcing me every time to have extra meal. She always used to say, "Some extra food won't harm you. You are growing up; this food will help you to be strong."

Now, in this desolated land, we were hunting for food; we were starving.

I stood with a stick beside Father trying to help him catch something from the river . . . eyeing on things travelling towards us. It was tiring to stand endlessly like Father possessed with indefinite patience.

I turned back to see what Chime was doing.

I stood stunned by what I saw. A gigantic shadow of Chime flecked rocky cave wall . . . she was seated on a rock like a queen on her throne, in the gloom of the cave, feeding the ants. Her motherly Goddess figure was taking care of tiny creatures.

As I walked up to her my shadow overlapped hers. I stood still blocking the path of light for a while, and then went ahead; my shadow then appeared tiny in front of her shadow. I became fascinated by her shadow on the wall. When she reached her hand out, shadow reached its hand out, when she wiggled her leg, shadow wiggled its leg. Light casted magic.

It captured Chime's curiosity.

Chime suddenly got up and yelled, "Brother, come here. Look . . ." Caravan of ants was marching towards her, up on the hilly road.

"Don't move Chime; stay still and look at the wall," I said. Without moving she watched her shadow.

Then I moved back slowly . . . shadow grew larger and larger as I was moving back. As I stepped away from the light, my shadow grew smaller.

Shadow game excited Chime. I asked her to feed the ants. She leant down to feed them.

The brighter the light, darker the shadow was.

I started feeding ants with Chime trying to make my shadow touch her hands without my hands actually touching. Then I asked her to stand up and raise hand towards the cave ceiling where algae had grown. She raised her hand up and her shadow touched the ceiling. She was delighted to see she managed to grab algae.

When she stood, I drew the due position with care, with a little ingenuity and some patience; I gave her a tail using my arm without touching her, making her look like an animal. New shadows appeared; she started giggling looking at her own animal like a shadow.

Inquisitive I wanted to add some more fun. Using my right hand, bending wrist I arched my fingers over a bit like a hook shape; taking my left hand and bringing it up towards my elbow I asked Chime to guess what the figure was.

She paused, thinking . . .

To give her a clue I started fanning my left hand and Chime exclaimed, "A bird!"

I took my ten fingers through various exercises before my bird took wings.

The duck quacked, donkey brayed, dog wagged his tail; infrequently, figures appeared on the wall that I never dreamt of attempting. It took all my brainpower to figure out how to make animals, birds; hand shadows tickled my brain.

I developed the hand ability to grasp the void.

Shadows sometimes were mystical, sometimes silent or sometimes frightening, too.

We had added feather to our monotonous life in the cave by inventing that magical play; a shadow play.

Something becomes nothing when a shadow is formed while everything becomes something. We were journeying into the dark, magical, mystical and enchanting domain of our Shadow!

'Shadow makes lonely company,' someone has said.

14

FIRST LEAF

Father was engaged in finding something edible; anything that could kill our hunger. Under the scalding sun, he stood on the edge of the river; anticipating, something would flow towards him. He was busy collecting twigs, leaves . . .

Proud of our invention, Chime and I were occupied with exploring new shadows; we whispered . . . argued . . .

Overhearing our conversation Father yelled, "Kaba, are you going to spend all your time playing? You have your books. Why don't you study? That will help you next year in the school and besides this, you can teach Chime; may be alphabets or numerical, whatever you learnt in your first year of the school."

Father, in his life never had seen school; he never learnt alphabets, numerical. But he knew the importance of education.

For me, it was a strenuous effort to study; my empty stomach didn't let my brain work. "May be trying to study will distract us from hunger" I thought; it was not a bad idea.

The best thing was Professor Charak was not around and I didn't have to stay away from Father and Chime for the sake of studies.

"Which subject should I study?" I wondered. I reached my sack to get the notebooks; English, Hindi, Social Science, General Science, Mathematics, *Bodhik*— Mother Tongue. I browsed through them all; my brain was dossing. I was not in the state of mind to play a brain game.

I picked up my notebook and pen; sitting before the Tree of Life I started thinking how to begin. I decided to make a timetable first; the one I always followed in the school. I realized we had no calendar to keep track of dates; the past ten days we counted on our fingertips. One by one I tried to count the days and failed to note them.

I glanced at the 'Tree' . . . Many thoughts harbored in my mind . . . I removed wax colors from my bag, picked an orange stick and started darkening the trunk Father had sketched with coal. I drew the very first leaf over it with green color and numbered it 'One': The day we were trapped in the cave; the day when *Chadar* refused to show us our path. Following number one, I added second . . . third . . . fourth . . . fifth . . . sixth . . . seventh . . . eighth . . . ninth . . .

"Brother, wait . . . I also want to add a leaf to the tree," Chime interrupted. She was willing to draw a leaf too; jumping around several times with a wax stick in her hand, she tried to reach the leafy part of the Tree on the wall. Her hand couldn't reach the top of the trunk.

When her jumping in the air didn't help, she said disappointedly, "Brother, I can't reach the tree."

I picked her up and she finally added a tenth leaf to the Tree. Those ten leaves indicated our past ten days we had spent in the cave; days filled with darkness, cold and hunger.

Eventually we learned to cope up finding a beautiful new oasis to call home.

I gestured at Father and Chime looking at the Tree, "From now on, we will add one leaf every day to this tree friend of ours," I said proudly.

I felt like the inventor of the calendar.

Looking at the numbers on the leaves Chime asked me impatiently, "When are you going to teach me, brother?"

"Now!" I replied. I decided to start with numerical. I tore one blank page from notebook and gave it to Chime with a pencil. First time Chime held a pencil to write something on paper.

Whenever I used to reach home from school during winter vacation, she would take all my pencils to scribble on the notebooks; on her demand Father used to bring notebooks for her.

On our first day of studies in the cave, I decided to teach her 'How to hold a pencil.'

I opened my two-sides, bright orange color pencil box; it had a glittering rainbow on top with my initials scribbled. A ruler, eraser, few pens, sharpener and pencils had made room inside that small box.

I gave one blue pencil to Chime.

"Hold it in your right hand," I said. She tried to hold it twisting her fingers . . . dropping the pencil several times . . . stretching her hand, and then shifted the pencil into her left hand.

"Chime, hold your pencil in your right hand," I said again.

Holding the pencil in left hand, she answered, "Brother, I can't write with my right hand; I simply can't hold the pencil."

"Can I use my left hand and write?" confused Chime asked me.

I nodded with approval.

She started her writing; first tracing broken horizontal lines, then vertical lines on the paper.

Her grip on the pencil was loose; I sat by her side. Keeping the notebook on my lap I held her left hand in my right hand and with pencil we slowly started writing on the paper; our fingers squashed into one another. First we drew a few straight lines . . . then slant and curve lines, followed by circles. The point of our pencil broke with the increased pressure. I always hated it when pencil leads broke.

I started sharpening the pencil trying to achieve the perfect point with a single-holed, red color plastic sharper. Sharpening the pencil was a rewarding experience for her. Her eyes were remarking my hands, carefully. Our pencil produced interesting blue rimmed, long curls shavings; pencil got a long and smooth point. She collected them, trying not to break them into bits.

She glued them like a circle on a piece of paper. She did three circles, made leaves and stem and we had three flowers!!! I had taught Chime this artwork some time back and was surprised to see she remembered it.

Her creativity enthralled me.

Squares, rectangles, triangles, circles resided in a notebook. I asked her to fill them with colors. And she did.

She enjoyed every moment and was willing to learn more.

We wrote one to ten numbers, pronouncing them loudly, so she could memorize them. Father was watching us from a distance. There was no courtyard, no lobby; neither timber—floor nor white painted mud rendered classroom. Chime learnt her first lesson in the cave under hazardous circumstances.

But her enthusiasm was unbridled; she was a quick learner.

We had been swallowed up into the darkness that gave no perception of visual; the grey lines on my notebook faded, suddenly the world closed in.

Chilly, damp moonlight enveloped the earth. Eleventh day passed. We were totally dependent on water. Father was not able to find anything solid. He had gathered some wooden spikes and thud; he spread them out on the rocks to dry, but nothing that we could eat.

Another night arrived with the darkness and bone-chilling cold. Filling our stomach with water, quickly we made our beds and tucked ourselves in our sleeping bags. Father looked exhausted and really worried. Discussing random things we went to bed. My mind harked back to the village; I thought of Maa, our home-the safest place on the earth.

Till now, I always thought Yoko was unlucky. He could never go to school. But when I slept in the cave, in the darkness I felt Yoko was luckier than me. At least he was safe and sound at his home.

Fear shivered through me; fear of not knowing the time span we had to spend in the cave without food, without fire.

Our energy drained enormously by now; but that day Tree of Life had shed rejuvenating 'Light' into the cave.

There is a saying in Tibetan: 'Tragedy should be utilized as a source of strength'—No matter what sort of difficulties, how painful experience is, if we lose hope, that is our real disaster.'

15

SENSE OF ISOLATION

Beneath a frigid dawn, Maa woke up every morning with the first stroke of the gong. Like Father, she would feed the yaks and milked them each day.

Her household life associated with intense labor; her days filled with agony . . .

Praying every day for half an hour was her routine; after prayers, like a ritual, she visited the banks of the river only to witness long ribbons of melting ice. Every day she visited river with hope and returned home disappointed.

Sometimes she spent her evenings curled up in one corner; she woke up at midnight to find herself alone in the room. Loneliness was her fate to be avoided.

She lurked into the darkness; the sense of isolation and loneliness crushed her. There was no other way to reach us . . . days faded . . . she was in quest of answers.

One day Maa decided to visit Haji's place along with Nyima aunty. During these days, Nyima aunty accompanied Maa like her shadow.

Passing through the valleys until she reached Haji's hut Maa was tense; an uncomfortable premonition of fear pervaded her senses.

She thought, "Would this meeting with Haji help her find all the answers she was seeking or they would lead her into an unreal world?" A world she couldn't dare to imagine. She kept asking Nyima Aunty, "Will Haji answer all my questions? Will she predict anything dissenting?"

Her thoughts twisted and turned like any path in the Zanskar valley . . . isolated . . . unchartered . . . no one really knows where the path is heading.

Her each step became heavier as she neared her destination; her thoughts choked. After a slogging walk, heavy heartedly, she finally reached Haji's place. Maa didn't dare to enter the hut or maybe she didn't wish to enter; she stood outside, frozen. Nyima aunty knocked the door.

Haji opened the door and let them in; she stared at Maa for long.

"Zampa you really look worried," taking Maa's hand in her hand, Haji said.

Haji sensed her trouble; she touched her nerve. It left her both intrigued and perplexed.

"You can handle trouble and carry heavy burden, Zampa. You have to keep your heart warm and smile on your face whenever you feel like screaming."

"The Believer of the almighty picks up the brick the devil throws on them and uses it as a strong foundation." Haji quoted.

Haji had read Maa's mind.

She then sat on her mat meditating; holding her rosary. Thoughts were rolling like waves in Maa's mind. Maa was seeking renewal of her restless soul.

She was eagerly waiting for Haji to finish her rituals.

"Yes, Zampa tell me what you want to know?" asked Haji.

"Haji, *Chadar* has melted. I am worried . . . are they safe? When will they return?" asked mother . . . choking. She had to be courageous to listen to Haji's predictions.

After blessing the rosary with suitable mantra, holding the rosary with index finger and thumb of left hand then going along a stretch of rosary with right hand she stopped at arbitrary spot; breathing heavily.

She counted the beads again . . . then paused. Seizing the beads in both hands Haji counted them the third time, analyzing.

Shading the light on mystery she answered, "God's help is at hand; they are under his shelter, have faith in him dear."

The answer lifted her spirit . . . Maa was speechless . . . her eyes filled with tears.

"Thank you so much Haji, I had been wandering through devil thoughts all these days," said Maa.

"Thank you Lord for listening to my prayers," she murmured.

Aunt Nyima was relieved too.

Receiving Haji's blessings both left from there. Mother was contented with the thought that she could expect our arrival any day. She was sure we would return one day.

Journeying in the deep stillness she was trying to weave an intricate web of her life.

16

MYSTERIOUS DOMAIN

E veryday wind howled as if whispering; talking to me in chant '*Chadar* would not form soon' and I believed. The sky forgot to change its color and faded into pale blue. Vicious Himalaya stood still blocking our path.

Days passed, we followed the same routine. We breathed cold air, drank water to fill our stomachs; fed our insect friends but we didn't have anything to eat.

Each passing day made us weaker. Chime lost her charm; her pink chubby cheeks looked sunken . . . her eyes never glittered.

Without food, we were running on empty stomach and our physical exertion consumed the energy. Our body was literally eating away our own muscles.

With folding hands, sometimes spreading forearms, fanning fingers, raising nails up, bending thumps down I created shadows of animals on the walls . . . goats, dogs, rabbits and elephants.

Sometimes a dog barked, fish swam, rabbit wiggled its ear and flower bloomed.

In the half-light of the gloomy cave we ventured into the dark shadow play to catch a smile that had long gone.

We were journeying into the mysterious domain of our life.

I tried to teach Chime as much as I could; she learnt numerical. I had started teaching her alphabets. Chime scribbled on almost all the pages of my notebook; only few blank pages left.

Father couldn't find any consumable organism; finding anything to eat could be a miracle.

All he could do was to gather the wooden thuds, spikes, grass. He always dried everything in sunlight. During the night, to save his gatherings from moisture he would then bring them inside the cave.

The nights were no longer colder and we could spend nights without fire but empty stomach bothered us awfully. Weakness constantly attacked us, not allowing us to sleep.

Every night before going to bed we prayed and then someone from us would draw the leaf, for every passing day, followed by Father or me giving it a number.

Each leaf indicated the end of a day on our Tree of Life.

The schedule didn't work for long as hunger strongly replaced our routine.

Life in the cave was like Zanskar River; it could freeze any moment as if it never existed or it could flow rapidly flaunting its presence. Every day our hunger was growing as high as the canyons in the Zanskar valley.

Human nature, created by God, hammered our thoughts and routine. I could rarely sleep, not longer than an hour at a stretch, even during nights. Apprehension and anxiety roused me. We barely slept.

Back home, whenever Maa woke me up early in the morning, I always wanted to stay in bed. And in the cave, I wanted to get out of the bed but I couldn't . . . simply because of hunger.

We could no more rely on water and desperately needed some solid food; our body had started giving up. We had the fuel but no food or organism. We were hungry. I thought about food obsessively.

My imagination was roaming unbridled. The one I had in the evening was more of a psychedelic kind.

Food portions were becoming larger and larger; my fantasy meals grew to the size of the whole Zanksar valley; from Zanskar to Ladakh. I dreamt whole river flowing outside cave was like soup, hot *momos* grew mountain size, bowls of *skiu* was like snow of the Himalayas, Sun was the fire and all the trees were fuel to cook the food.

My dreaming became quiet expert; all ingredients for my dishes were always fresh and plenty in supply. My stove 'Sun' was always at the right temperature . . . there were enough trees to fuel it. The proportion of the things was always banged on. Nothing was ever burnt or undercooked, nothing too hot or too cold. Every meal was simply perfect. Only, it was beyond reach.

By degrees the range of my appetite increased. I wished if I could fly like a dragon. I would have transformed myself into a giant who could fill the entire sky and grab the *momos*. I would have drunk my soup.

I got attached to my mental phenomena, believing it's real.

But Reality was an enemy.

After a week, fatal weakness started creeping upon us. That was the time anything was good to eat, no matter whatever the taste was. I was so hungry that I could put anything in my mouth, chew it and swallow it—delicious, foul or plain.

I can still remember a moment of insanity that brought by hunger. We were more keen eating than staying alive and the every passing day slowly did the job of unbending our strength.

It is pointless to say, this or that night was the worst of my life. I have so many bad nights to choose; I made none the champion.

That entire week was the maximum period we had spent without any solid intake. When I think back, I can hardly believe it myself that how we survived those days.

17

TIMELESS ILLUSIONS

We had pursued our journey on the ice track on 29th January; for three days we walked, shuffled, slipped, climbed, waded, grunted and belly crawled our way into Zanskar.

Sometimes we travelled at river level and sometimes climbed high above the cliff; on the flat, slippery surfaces. We waded through the water, through hundreds of ice chips, over ice that was thankfully very much solid.

We walked safely through *'The Land of Mystic Lamas'*, through *'The Land of the Last Shangri-La'*; we spent restful nights during these three days walk.

After three tiresome days, we refuge in the cave until we realized we were trapped by the world's mightiest mountain ranges, the Greater Himalayas and by the mysterious Zanskar River.

We were Isolated; away from our homeland, away from my mother.

Our journey of Zanskar valley had started on 29th of January but I feel the journey of our life started on 1st of February; from the first day we entered the cave for shelter.

For me, the very first leaf of our Tree of Life therefore, signifies 1st February.

The days were long and grueling; we survived on Tiffin for ten days and each bite consumed the probability of our survival in the cave.

The struggle for survival started from the tenth leaf onwards when there was absolutely no food.

I picked up my red wax stick, when I got up, I felt tingling on my fingertips and toes; I felt like passing out, flushed. With shaky hands, I added seventeenth leaf to our Tree; as I did, I realized it had been seven days . . . we lived without solid food.

Our entire journey was now against time; the way through which we had to travel was 'TIME'. Time baffled us; governed everything in us.

I doubted the nature of existence. By examining the present, we couldn't predict the absolute certainty what would happen in future; future was mere the hidden present.

Our companions were 'HOPE', 'STRENGTH', 'FAITH' and 'TOGETHERNESS'. There were many hurdles in our journey, more than Zanskar valley and the most important hurdle to go through was 'HUNGER'.

Our 'JOURNEY' started from the cave and now, our destination was no more to reach Ladakh School but 'SURVIVAL'. We had to pass the time against all odds to reach there.

It was a mental journey than physical; we had to take courageous challenges at every step.

We still had a long way to travel. Without food we couldn't cope with it and reach our target of survival.

The pain was quiet excruciating. We were becoming weaker, confused and slower day by day.

Only seventeen days passed so far and our companions 'HOPE', 'STRENGTH', 'FAITH' was leaving us.

I still remember the words; a very important lesson for life Father told me that night about different types of people.

He said, "Kaba, some people give up on life with only a resigned sigh. Others fight a little and then lose hope. Still others and we are one of those who will never give up. We will fight and fight and fight. We fight no matter the cost of battle, the losses we face, the improbability of success. We fight to the very end and complete the journey; journey of our life. It's not a question of courage. It's something constitutional, an inability to let go. It may be nothing more than life—hungry stupidity."

25th Leaf:

We had been hungry for fifteen days. It is difficult to evaluate which week was more crucial and unforgettable, first or second?

As second week passed, hunger took a toll on us, we panicked and to ignore it was highly impossible.

The permanence and eternity and the resulting denial of change in the *Chadar* caused an illusion.

Illusion was a space we were wandering through aimlessly, against limitless reality.

18

HUNGRY DEVILS

Leaf 26.
I was immobile in the morning; weakness pinned me to the bed. I tried to think about the days we spent in the cave; but to apply myself to think straight exhausted me. My head was spinning; white swirls surrounded me.

The sense of self was hard-wired; I believed that my soul left my body, I felt threatened.

We had lost lots of weight and day-by-day we were turning into skeletons. Chime's body emaciated; her shiny hair turned into a coil, her lips chapped; she looked dreadful. Little by little she started loosing interest in studies. There were days when she glued to her 'Chime Land' for hours and hours; staring at the floor when spoken to 'like she didn't even hear you . . . like she was in her own world.'

With a growing beard and sloppy hair, Father transformed from a man into an ape. He'd had only one blanket to cover him for a month; his muddied *goncha* tattered. He resembled the caveman in my History textbook. His body consumed himself.

Each moment brought us closer to the finality of life; death was a matter of time.

I could feel the inside world of my stomach twisting and growling; demanding solid food constantly.

Chime called me; I looked around in a daze; I neglected her.

She called me again. "Brother, uncle Tsering has come; look there . . ." Pointing at the cave entrance she uttered, "Uncle Kalden is with him too."

I looked at the entrance but couldn't see anyone.

"Uncle is saying *Chadar* is frozen. Spirits in the valley have listened to our prayers; they have sent him here to save us . . ."

Seated in her corner, Chime extended her hand towards me and said, "Hurry up brother, don't waste time, we have to cover a very long distance . . ."

I was bewildered; I didn't trust her words.

I walked further feeling stiff. Clutching my blanket for warmth, wearily, struggling with my left over strength in my body, I advanced towards the entrance; neither uncle Tsering was there nor porter Kalden. I bent down on my knees to touch the icy trail. *Chadar* was not frozen . . .

Chime started walking towards the edge of the river; she kept murmuring, "Hurry up brother . . . we are going to see Maa . . ."

Father approached, seeing her walking towards the flowing river. He shook her hard and eventually brought her back to reality.

I couldn't understand her behavior. Everything got flashy, shadowy and hurt my head.

She was hallucinating.

The torture of my fear threatened to crush me.

Father was frightened and wanted to protect us from the harshness and disappointments.

I spotted his bony figure standing by the riverside every day; hoping to catch something eatable. He continued with his daily routine, ignoring the pain he pushed himself hard; but despite his best efforts, our conditions worsened.

If anyone had asked me to cross the Zanskar valley again, I would have done that. I am sure, it couldn't be stressful than getting out of the bed and walking further five steps inside the cave; it was a hell of a thing to realize.

We hovered between life and death. Our condition had deteriorated to such an extent that, for us, immediate survival became a priority than long-term survival.

Chime fed her ant friends regularly despite being weakened but she never seemed happy or excited.

I don't know from where she gained so much energy to feed the ants in such utmost conditions. She was more tolerant than me.

In the fight against hunger she was a better warrior than me.

I guess it was just her friends who distracted her from thoughts of hunger and because of the distraction; her condition was a little better than mine. Other factor that helped her was she didn't have the ability to think for a long-term result.

Devoid of all deep and prolonged thoughts she lived in the present and any small thing could easily put her thoughts at bay.

We had companions for the rest of the travelling, only time could tell us whether they were temporary or permanent accompanies; 'WEAKNESS', 'HUNGER', 'HALLUCINATION', sometimes 'BOREDOM' too.

Life rolled on in the strange and timeless land.

I questioned the Almighty, "Why you are not listening to our prayers? What is our destiny? Why can't you change our destiny for its better?" My subconscious cried in vain.

One thing I realized during these suffocating days, my Father was certainly a better man than anyone else. He was trapped in a cave with his children. What would be his priority?

Firstly, he would do his best for his children to keep them safe and alive. He couldn't give up because of his children. The only thing destiny allowed him to do was try his best and he was trying his best; but this was due to his emotional bonding with us.

He was not only a father but also a human being. "How long could he survive against these harsh, life threatening circumstances? Doesn't he feel like shedding off his responsibilities as a father and run away?" my numb brain asked me.

I started thinking of the paths Father could have lead at his worst.

1. He could jump into the river with both of us; a suicide attempt.
2. He could have killed us predicting further suffering leading towards a miserable end.
3. At worst to worst extent he could have made us his meal; like the famous Zanskari story of King Gyapos: while crossing *Chadar* along with his courtiers and cook, he was stuck inside the cave

just like us for night halt and *Chadar* vanished unexpectedly the next day. They waited for many days but condition didn't change; there was no escape. When their food stock finished, the king along with the courtiers secretly decided to kill the cook for food. Overhearing them, the cook sat on the banks of the river and prayed to God . . . and the next morning *Chadar* was formed.

That could have been one of the probabilities of what a human can attempt for survival, maybe for a cave men or apes too.

But we were luckier in that sense because Father didn't turn into a CANNIBAL!

Chime's luckier friends were filling their tiny stomachs with algae. Algae layered inside and outside the cave.

Father noticed tiny creatures surviving on algae . . .

Father scratched and collected some algae from the rocks of the cave and filled our Tiffin boxes, and then he washed it clean.

Algae with its strange pungent smell could only be food for microorganisms. I could have never imagined algae as a food for us.

No shame, no foul if you try something once and survive; and we did.

You never know what will save you. Food existed in the cave but we never spotted. That moment taste of the food didn't matter.

We were not at the Monastery Festival to enjoy the feasts of the substantial amount of *Dresi, Skiu, Thukpa, Droma, and Kapse*.

At that moment algae was the only possible dish . . .

If we could digest algae as food, then we might be saved. No matter the taste, slowly, in a few days, we would get used to the smell and the taste.

We sat around the Tiffin; without giving any second thought Father took a very first bite of algae.

"Kaba, Chime, eat it," he stated seriously.

Chime looked impassively from Father to me.

"What?" She questioned.

I knew it would be hard for her to eat algae but I couldn't wait to decide; my inside was yelling at me, "Eat it . . . eat it . . . this is the only food available in this secluded place; you must eat for survival."

I plunged my fingers into the mossy green algae; it slipped through my fingers; I hesitated for a moment. But to encourage Chime, I grabbed it with all my five fingers; and clinching eyes tight, quickly I had a bite.

Chime was staring at me, gauging my reaction.

To my surprise, it was not as bad as I had imagined. It tickled my tongue, I didn't have to chew it; I simply swallowed.

The taste was like raw grinded vegetables. I still have the taste of my first bite of algae still lingers on my taste buds.

Father finally discovered the food . . . the solid intake. I felt as if I was seeing the food first time in my lifetime.

I could feel the energy flowing inside me with that single bite of algae. We both looked at Chime, hoping she would eat it.

She timidly looked at our face.

"I can't eat this, Father," she said, her voice low. She couldn't bring herself to actually bite into the algae.

I don't know what bothered her the most; the color of algae, its texture or smell?

Father said, "If your insect friends can eat this food, then why not you? If you can't have this then you should not feed your friends. This will give you energy to stand up and walk around. You will be able to study with Kaba if you eat this food."

I blinked up at her. "Eat it, Chime. It's not bad; it doesn't taste different than *Tsampa,* its just looking green," I requested.

For a while she observed the Tiffin filled with algae and then dug her fingers into it; her tiny, little fingers layered with algae, she squirmed uncomfortably.

"Close your eyes and eat it, Chime," I encouraged her. Breathing heavily, she closed her eyes; opening the mouth wide she put her fingers in her mouth and gulped the algae; she immediately took a sip of water.

Initial bites were a bit difficult for her, she made faces while eating; but after two to three bites we emptied all our Tiffin. It felt as if the devil of hunger that had been yelling inside my stomach for something solid was suppressed by the algae intakes.

Our taste buds had accepted algae, so Father scraped off some more and filled our Tiffin; he washed it with fresh river water and we happily ate it.

A Great saying written on our monastery wall, taught by the monks to the people of Zanskar for living in the strangest conditions secluded from the outside world: 'It is not the strongest of the species that survives, nor the most intelligent; it is the one who is the most adaptable to change.'

And we had followed the great words on inspiration, adapting to change.

We accepted the conditions and ate something unusual and raw.

Night crept in; our surroundings disappeared into eerie darkness.

But my mind and soul were filled with brightness because we struggled and had crossed one of the biggest ledges of our journey.

Though it was a temporary solution for our hunger, as long as it saved us, it didn't matter. We were not in a position to think about and choose our needs. For us algae was the best food in the world.

Our presence was manifested by the power of our belief and our deep rapport with God.

19

CHURNING THOUGHTS

With rising temperature nature enlivened shading its white clothes . . . dressing in greens.

Mother was facing the worst of nightmares. She didn't talk much; the words had gone . . . dissolved . . . they were out of reach. She was more than discouraged.

The only place she visited was Haji's house during the late hours of the day. Aunt Nyima took care of her and accompanied her most of the times. Even if Maa stayed till late in the evening at Haji's place, Nyima aunty stayed with her and accompanied back home late night. Every day Aunt Nyima cooked food at our place for my mother and left it in the tiffin.

Maa made it a habit to eat food late in the night. There were times she skipped it.

The routine couldn't stretch for long.

One evening Yoko was waiting for his mother along with his father, still she hadn't reached home. They went to our place to find her but she wasn't there. They waited for a long time.

By the time Maa and aunt reached home it was very late. Uncle Lobsang warned her saying not to waste time being with my mother all the time.

He said to her, "I never stopped you to come here, but you should not forget, you also have a family and some responsibilities."

Then he told Maa, "Zampa, I feel sorry for you but *Chadar* will not form sitting on its bank for hours neither visiting Haji. We can't go against nature. Haji can only predict things but she can't give any solution. I don't see *Chadar* forming so soon. You may have ample of time on your hand because Norbu and children are not home. But Yoko's mother has. She will not go with you tomorrow onwards."

He portrayed harsh reality . . . reality that pierced her very bones.

Before leaving he said, "Zampa, I can only hope for the best . . . whenever *Chadar* forms Norbu and children will come back. But you should prepare yourself for the worst. You should learn to take care of yourself . . . and your yaks.

We will be there with you if you need any help . . . life doesn't stop . . . learn to move on."

They left. Embraced by the wilderness she stood rooted to the ground. Her eyes fixed somewhere in the distance.

Maa knew that her best friend had done whatever she could. She too had a family . . . she was a woman too.

Dark clouds seemed to constantly loom over her head.

After that night aunt Nyima stopped visiting my place. Thereon Yoko started bringing Tiffin for Maa.

Yoko's parents paid casual visits but as days passed those casual visits faded.

Maa cleared her mind. Her routine changed besides her visits to Haji's place; the only place she found peace.

With the lengthening of twilight shadow, she was getting up with the first stroke of the gong.

Winter had disappeared in the melting snow. The nights were no longer cold to keep the yaks inside the room. The day started breaking earlier, so the timing of the gong was altered consequently.

She had made it a pattern to milk yaks then to clear yaks' dung and make dung cakes for fuel. Father's saved fodder ran out; Maa had to take the yaks to the fields for grazing.

Afternoon shadows started stretching long and thin. Wandering through the fields yanking the yaks, directing them Maa used to climb up through the alpine meadows for three four hours daily, late in the afternoon their caravan used to return home.

From a world of swirling white she descended into a world of green.

She opened the warehouse after a month. The warehouse was dead silent except for the intermittent creaks; weeds and dandelions poked out from those cracks. The darkness in the warehouse encased Maa. The distinctive odor of cheese and butter filled in the air. The mud walls showed brown blotches, caused by neglect. Cobwebs covered the corners of the doors, shelves, logs of the ceiling . . . so as her thoughts.

Maa cleaned the warehouse on her own. Preparing cheese kept her busy. More than churning of the butter, it seemed she churned her thoughts for hours and hours to kill the time.

Every evening after cheese making she visited Haji to regain the faith she had in supreme power. While returning from Haji's house collecting the Tiffin daily from Yoko's house was part of her routine; she had to because she was left with no staple.

Trying all possible ways to stay occupied and not to think about us was a task for her or else hollowness in her life would have either killed her or led her to madness.

In that quiet, empty space she tried to sleep, but her sleeping patterns changed. She had fitful sleep; any sound could awake her many nights, reminding her about us.

Her nights were always long, haunted by lost empire.

One day, at dawn, chasing the swift wind, descending into the green oasis Maa reached the *Karsha* monastery.

She journeyed all alone in the mountainous land.

It was bright and sunny by the time Maa reached monastery; she approached a monk and gave him some butter as an offerings.

Bowing against him she said, "I am here to perform a prayer . . . for safety of my family and their longevity . . . they are on their way to Ladakh and *Chadar* has melted . . .

Something in her stirred with a deep yearning.

I am worried for them." She choked.

The monk absorbed her thoughts; he asked Maa to wait in the prayer hall and walked back to one of the chambers.

Maa waited in the prayer hall; the atmosphere reverberated with the sounds of '*Om Mani Padme Hum*', monks recited the mantras in unison.

After a while, the monk returned with a bundle of *'Lung-ta'*—the five colored prayer flags.

He guided Maa up the way to mountainside; following him through pebbled lanes she reached the mountaintop.

Monk burnt the incense stick onto hot coals; then offered green juniper branches, some aromatic medicinal saps and herbs to the wood fire.

Maa observed his every action; she was not in her element.

The aromatic smoke was offered to local deities . . . to the beings of all the realms. He then recited *'Sampa Lhundrup'*—Wish Fulfilling Prayer and *'Barche Lamsel'*—a powerful prayer of *'Guru Padmasambhava'* to clear the obstacles in our path. He passed the folded prayer flags through the smoke and then hoisted them high for the wind to carry the beneficent vibrations for our longevity.

The flag shredded by the wind: the blue flag with imprinted *'Amitayus'*—*Buddha* of Limitless Life swayed for our health and longevity. The *'Wind Horse'* on the white flag along with *Garuda*—a supernatural eagle, dragon, tiger and snow lion galloped like a wind towards the four corners of the earth, carrying blessings for us. *'Guru Rinpoche'* with *'Vajra'*—thunderbolt in his right hand sat with the 'wish fulfilling prayer' on the red flag, subduing the negative forces. To protect us from all dangers *'White Tara'*—mother of all Buddha's resided on the Green flag. *'Sitatapatra'*—white umbrella; the dome of the sky stood high on the yellow flag, casting its shadow on us to protect from illness and natural calamities.

The natural energy of the wind gently harmonized the surroundings.

Maa's companions . . . her only hope, were these supreme deities: *Amitayus, Wind Horse, Guru-Rinpoche, White Tara* and *Sitatapatra.*

She believed the powerful spiritual energy would increase the good fortune and happiness.

Standing against the flags, she prayed silently; hoping the wind would touch us with sacred symbols and mantras and uplift our spirits; her prayer dissipated and rose to heaven.

20

TOGETHER

Leaf 34.
Gleaming sunlight peeked through the cave for longer time; blowing fresh breeze grazed our faces. River murmured mildly. Brown headed gulls occasionally flew by over the sea chirping loudly; sometimes landing, floating smoothly on the sea for a while . . . soon disappearing back into the canyons.

Cave regained her life, she smelt fresh; tiny yellow, blue flower buds peeped through the rocks to greet Mother Earth.

Life was blooming recklessly outside the cave. Healing green leaves were waving at us. The noontime air was warm and steamy but evenings were always chilly.

To spring up our life in the cave, I continued teaching Chime.

It was early afternoon; Chime, as usual sat beside me with a pencil in her left hand, notebook on her lap. With a blunt pencil point she was struggling to write one to ten digits, talking aloud. One, two, three, four, five, seven . . . She paused looking at me and then continued in a confused state seven, six, eight, nine, and ten!

She exclaimed as if she crossed a hurdle; expecting appraisal she looked at me.

I said, "Chime, it's one, two, three, four, five, six, seven not seven, six, eight; all right? Repeat it."

She nodded sadly.

To encourage Chime Father said, "Let's repeat it together Chime. One, two, three, four . . ."

Chime said it aloud excitedly, "One, two, three, four . . ."

And together they said it aloud, "five, six, seven, eight, nine, ten!" Their voice echoed in the cave; it seemed cave was repeating numbers after them.

I had taught Father to write the digits up until ten . . .

One to ten digits were initially difficult for him, but as he managed to by heart them; he learnt the trick to write the further numbers.

Verbally so far, he had managed to memorize pronouncing the numbers up to twenty, that's why he was trying to help and remind Chime whenever she fumbled.

Father and I expected Chime to pronounce the numbers in correct order; and often she ended up saying one, two, three, five, four, six, seven . . . !

During our tutorial sessions Chime always answered like a pin puncturing a balloon, popping the bubble of silence that inhabited our monotonous lives in the cave.

I experienced these pleasurable moments in the isolated land because 'We were TOGETHER'.

Our togetherness helped us survive through the hell like situation.

I imagined my life in the cave without Father and Chime; and all I could see myself facing 'Yama'; who holds the Wheel of Life in his hooves—the Lord of the Hell Realm.

Surely, I would already have been dead in their absence.

It was company . . . Chime's company that kept us engaged in silly talks and strange activities. Chime was casting a magical spell on us like a 'Dakini'—an angel. Chime was a blessing.

Seeing Chime fighting with hunger more bravely than me, gave me strength; I was her teacher in the cave, if I would have given up, then what would I have taught her? I tolerated every situation because I didn't want to be a loser.

Every little boy or girl has a guardian Angel at his side . . . ours was Father. It was Father's company that never left us alone; that gave me strength.

We had a powerful protector who was taking care of us.

He navigated us through Zanskar valleys and now through the valleys of Life too.

Like God, he was the thread between life and death that kept us woven and granted life to move on.

Father was struggling hard to fulfill our every basic necessity our existence demanded. He kept us alive serving algae; and that day, since morning seated on a rock, he was trying to source the fire.

Fire, the basic need, could change our life for better.

Curiously, Chime and I moved towards him to see what our Father was innovating exactly.

Placing a small ball of tinder in front he began to scratch one small stone against the rocky wall of the cave to create the spark by trying all possible frictions to achieve fire. Chime and I observed his every move with interest. He changed his position many times; sometimes kneeling on the floor . . . sometimes sitting on the floor . . . holding the stone in various angles and without slowing down he tried various unsuccessful attempts.

I realized starting fire by using friction was the greatest gift to man from his Creator; the biggest discoveries on the planet. But it was not easy as one thinks.

We had experienced the life without fire over a month, and learnt the important role of fire.

Absence of fire had darkened our world; we suffered the chilling temperatures of the Himalayas shivering, our body went numb for several nights. We ate anything in its raw state just to keep ourselves alive. The life we were leading was an animal life without fire.

Today, when I look back with a different perspective, then I realize, in a way we were luckier. GOD had chosen us to experience the primitive life. From humans we were transformed into apes and from apes we were evolving back to humans.

In a way, we were retrograded from this modern world to the Paleolithic era and the otherwise, following rules of evolution.

In one life we had seen the whole world and the existence of humans. In a way we were the world setter.

Despite of whole days enduring trials to create a fire, unfortunately, Father couldn't achieve a single spark. He didn't give up; he had decided to meet the God of fire.

For many days he kept on rubbing, scraping, stacking something then stooping . . . experimenting to produce the fire somehow; nothing worked. He was not an expert at producing fire, what he gained in return of his efforts was some blisters on his palms.

His trials failed. Father tried to find as many different types of stones as possible.

He picked up stones buried in the ground. Chime and I gathered various types of stones considering they might be the right ones. They varied in textures, shapes; shades: dark-green, soft white, hard grey, pale yellow, sharp brown; stones from the cave, stones from the river. We collected all.

Father tried applying new techniques and new ways to hold the stones, but none of the combinations or techniques helped him achieve expected results. He could never attempt the actual technique needed.

Then he expanded on the idea that each location offered different characteristics. Perhaps the weather had a profound effect on the texture or even the hardness of the stones. He tried to take into account just about every factor he could think of.

After many variations, techniques and combinations, I actually started to believe that it couldn't be achieved. It was nothing but a waste of energy for us. But the positive side was that it kept us busy for many days, we spent ample of our time on this activity, so time passed by quickly.

We were mentally and physically engaged in it.

Besides, I never forgot to draw a leaf on our tree with every passing day. The Tree of Life was growing bigger and leafy.

Chime sometimes felt bad for her tiny friends that we were eating their food. I was worried thinking what would she feed them once we would finish all the algae?

An alga has a nature to regenerate itself; we hoped we would not run out of the stock.

Eating raw algae desensitized the taste goblet. My taste buds needed refinement. I wished, some day Father would catch some fish or any water organism. I didn't know how it would taste but I assumed it would definitely be better than the tasteless raw algae.

The ferociously flowing, freezing cold river never allowed any organism to survive or flow in our direction.

I hoped with the rising temperature and change in the climatic conditions, someday a treat by God would come our way.

Father shared his thoughts and stone striking activities with us. He learnt that lot of his activities emerged through his various experiments crafted his knowledge about fire. He was learning through his experience so far but nothing sparked.

Figuring his skills was hopeless in finding the answer for the fire. He had moved back to his previous work of gathering twigs and sticks, dividing them by size, sorting out softwood, juniper branches whatever he was collecting from the flowing river; still waiting for some organism to flow. Our fate served us just wooden twigs and spikes which, were of no use to us unless we had a fire . . .

21

WELCOMING GUEST

Sun poured through the valleys; sitting at the edge of the river Father and I were talking about something unimportant.

While talking he asked me to wait . . . something had struck him; something that made him stop and think.

Trying to remember, he discussed some of the problems he had come across in trying to develop his 'two stones' technique.

He said, "Our stones were always flashing, but with no real spark, and the dirt that had accumulated on the tinder was so heavy that the tinder would not catch a spark."

He chose two stones of almost the same size, used one of them as a striker, and the other one as static base-stone. Then he carved a groove carefully in the center of the base-stone, it appeared as a 'U' shaped hard shell.

While stroking the stones, with excitement he explained, "Pay attention Kaba, now I am carving the groove at this base-stone deeper; and by doing this I can focus more on the spark, not anywhere else."

The smaller angled but more defined channel seemed to give good results. He then kept the small portion of tinder in between the groove.

Maintaining the pressure, he stroked it as fast as he could create friction. Checking the groove he said, "This method may take less effort to get a spark and I don't have to strike the stone many times. It allows more life to the base-stone as well as protects longevity of the striker."

I noticed that with less impact on the stones, there was less debris being transferred to our tinder.

"Remember Kaba, this was our one of the major concerns in the past; our tinder was so dirty that even a matchstick would hardly light it. Making these changes to the base-stone we now have a cleaner surface area to accept the sparks and by having the deeper channel, it directs more of the sparks to the waiting tinder," Father explained.

The deeper channel had an advantage.

It allowed for more wind protection after striking the stones, thus sheltering the spark, giving the maximum opportunity for the spark to get hotter.

The longevity of the striker had a lot to do with the pattern; several times he'd had to improve it and re-craft other strikers.

Talking like a scientist he said, "Now I understand the reasons why I didn't get any sparks with the earlier techniques. My idea of striking two same stones together was not practical. True, I got the ember but nothing at the temperature to create a spark. By using a striker which has a greater hardness than the base-stone, the impact of striking these two stones together will send a spark from the stones to the tinder."

Understanding the many mistakes he had committed and learning from them, he was using this new technique. We could see his confidence and excitement.

Chime and I joined him; our curiosity was cast in bronze.

Father was very much confident it would work. To my surprise, it was working! The stone was getting hot with every stroke.

While striking the stones he said, "It seems really easy. Why was it so hard for me to accomplish it before?"

With a yearning desire, we looked at Father's hands, which were working rapidly; to and fro like a machine . . . the striking sound of the stones was pumping my adrenaline . . . with every stroke my heart beat faster.

I was eagerly awaiting the result; it was a goosebump situation for us. Father kept going on, switching his hands; he knew he couldn't stop. All his hard work could go in vain even if he stopped for a few seconds and the rising heat would drop off.

The heat between the stones increased, Father couldn't hold the base-stone as it got hot. Focusing on the base-stone Father said, "Kaba, quickly give me some paper or cloth."

I dashed towards my bag and tore a sheet of paper hurriedly from my notebook and handed it over to him. I didn't want to miss a single moment; he was holding the base stone using the paper as a guard to protect his hands from the heat. We could see his speed developing . . . his hands becoming red and sore. It was like a race for him . . . his hands were running . . . no matter what they had to win. We were very close to meet our new guest . . .

Almost after half an hour or so, we spotted thin coils of smoke emerging through the stones . . . this was a positive indication; we were about to welcome our guest!

The pain Father might be going through was unthinkable, since he had been rubbing the stones constantly . . . origin of the smoke made the pain forgettable at least for the time being.

The smoke was getting brighter . . . just a few more strokes . . . we were very much closer . . . he couldn't afford to stop. My pulse raced with enthusiasm and my heart beat faster than the monastery drums.

The moment he felt smoke was sufficient enough to move to the next step, he stopped rubbing and very carefully transferred the smoky dry grass to the waiting tinder. He already had a nest ready, made up of dry grass and dry leaves.

Now, all he needed to do was to add air. Fanning with his right hand he started feeding air to the smoke . . . it was a bright, intense glow, which we could see and then it evaporated. He leaned forward and blew on it gently, holding back and aiming the stream of air from his mouth to hit the brightest spot. Five or six blows had fallen on the tight mass of tinder. Father elevated his efforts at this point. One wrong step could easily destroy all his prior efforts. He had dedicated too much time to it and he couldn't bear starting over again.

The smoke grew with his gentle breath.

The waiting moment for all of us was over when he ran out of breath and paused to inhale; suddenly a red ball ignited, flames erupted and light filled the cave.

"Fire!" he yelled. "We've got fire! We've got it . . . we've got it . . . we've got it!" Chime's squinty eyes widened with excitement . . . Father's voice bore happiness and success. "Kaba, Chime it worked!" . . . He jolted.

We were overjoyed with arrival of fire. Chime and I jumped up and shouted with joy.

It was surely a big achievement and we were so proud of Father for his success. It was a life-changing discovery.

That was the best day I remember, in the cave and one which gave us so much happiness and a reason to survive.

But the flames were thick; they burnt and consumed the tinder nest as if gasoline were being used. Father had to feed the flames to keep them going. Working promptly, he carefully placed the dried grass and wood pieces; his stock gathered from the river for the past month would be enough for fuel.

He could not let the flames go out and kept adding tinder.

He collected most of the wooden twigs, spikes and fed the hungry flames. We helped him to put other stuff in the fire to keep it alight.

We had a hungry visitor friend with us, but a good one . . . 'FIRE'.

It was so precious; the yellow and red flames were brightening the dark interior of the shelter. The happy crackle of the burning dry wood was the best piece of music that played with our eardrums, giving never-ending pleasure and peace to our souls.

It was time for celebration.

We all sat in front of fire and Father let us pray to the fire God for coming and residing in our cave. Then he placed two stones near the fire and made a small traditional stove to put a container on.

I filled the container with river water and he put it over the stove. The water started boiling.

We scraped the algae, I washed it clean and Father added all the algae in the water. Algae boiled with water, and we all had hot algae soup, which was definitely better than raw algae.

Ultimately, we gained a change in the taste, leaving the raw taste behind; one more step in our successful evolution from caveman to human.

It seemed our ' Tree Of Life' was smiling and celebrating with us opening wide arms with a pulsating radiance.

That night, fire was a treat for us; it kept the cave warm and settled us back into the routine sleep. I fell fast asleep that night.

The fire had burned down to embers around midnight. The next morning, Father stirred the ashes with a piece of wood and found a bed of fuel and some stones still glowing hot and red. With small pieces of wood he carefully blew the fire and he soon had a blaze going again.

Father was not concerned about keeping the fire going on and lighting it unnecessarily all the time, wasting the fuel.

He knew the technique . . . it demanded more time to light initially but he was sure with more practice, he could achieve it someday.

I added the leaf numbering it sixty; I colored it in red and wrote 'FIRE' above it.

On the sixty fourth day, which was two months after nature had trapped us, we had all the 'F's necessary for our survival: 'Food, Fuel and Fire' and yes, fresh water and fresh air we already had as the gift of God.

22

MEMORABLE MARKERS

*A*fter the sixty fourth leaf until I added leaf number 180.

Four months; time was like a magician playing its tricks. It changed spring into summer, summer invited rain.

If I look back, I feel as if, yes, our survival was alchemic. I don't even remember how we jumbled those four months.

Was it a time lapse? Or simply, blank pages of a book I flipped through? Because no matter whatever happened, life kept on breathing, some desires emerged and hunger churned inside whether we liked it or not.

We lived in illusion and the appearance of things. The status of reality couldn't be applied to the self; we were nothing but everything.

Life never paused; it just bewitched our breaths.

We existed without living. Did the good spirits help us? Did White Tara bestow her blessings upon us? Or was it a magic of time?

Time has dimmed my memories of those days; what I can think of are the events, encounters, routines and markers that were etched on the trunk of our tree; just like special days highlighted in red on our annual calendar. Portraying leaves on the tree was illusionary during these days.

One of the memorable markers:

FISHING BY FATHER

His way of catching fish was simple; his weapon to hunt the fish was my red sack. Father had been using my sack as a trap but so far he had succeeded only in gathering some inedible materials from the river, still no eatable was found.

My sack was deep enough to keep all my books, clothes and food. It was like a trekking bag, sufficient enough to carry material for long distance journeys.

He cut all the unnecessary yellow straps that were hanging from its corners, and tied all of them with the center strap making it look like a conical float. He pinned the bottom of my sack and made several holes to make a way for water.

Father dropped this trap daily into the water waiting for fish to swim into it. Holding the strap of the float in his hand he stood on the edge of the river, the trap always floating.

Father's daily standing position appeared like a painting on canvas to me. Like a painting time had stood still for.

I had never seen fishing in my life nor did my Father try it any time before.

He waited . . . and waited . . . and waited.

The sun decided to show its exuberant face but not a single fish swam into our trap. The float was always dancing on the waves.

For the last few days of summer, a long tropical rain spell kept the skies cloudy, rendering the atmosphere gloomy and dismal keeping the temperatures down.

The crystal clear blue water was now rough and murky making it difficult for fish to see the lure.

During those days, Father was accustomed to staying in the river without venturing out beyond a certain point.

I can never forget the look of failure, the look of disappointment on his face.

FIRST FISH

One day, sitting on the rock I was mocking the river; ritually, Father had stood in the river with his float.

To our surprise, one fish swiftly entered the trap. Father was all excited so was I. I exclaimed with joy, "Father, fishhh!"

He tightened the strap hastily by pulling the float towards him and tried to hold the fish tightly in his hands. But its slipperiness made it a bit harder to get a grip; it wriggled and wrangled its way out of his hands, plopping back into the river.

Splashing, as if saying, "You can't catch me."

Father's red face rendered his anger.

He was certainly not about to give up. Seated beneath the blanket of the stars, he reinvented his fishing trap. Tying all the dry branches, sticks into bundles, he placed them upright on the bottom of the bag so the fish could get trapped easily.

'One more cast' is sometimes responsible for turning a slow day into a great day.

Next morning, light winds allowed the river water to turn flat and clear. Pale sunlight had filtered through smoky grey clouds.

Father again stood, hauling the trap into the river; more confident than the other days.

I began to get bored with the whole idea of waiting so I decided to help Father.

A few black—necked cranes forged in a small group, one bird acting as a sentinel. Seeing the cranes feeding very actively on fish, Father thought he might have a good chance of catching some.

I was standing behind Father to help him, this time more alert; we didn't want to lose any other fish.

The cool wind swirled around me; it was calming and exhilarating. Stricken into silence I stood for a long time along with Father.

I saw a fish passing by my feet, I felt like catching it with my bare hands.

Father spoke gently, "Stay still, Kaba. Don't move or else you will scare the fish."

He remained watchful, scanning through the river.

The fish was swirling around my feet; the ripples in the water tickled me. But I had to stay still.

In my mind, I was requesting fish, "Please, enter the trap . . . please . . . please." Holding my breath I was watching it; our food was so close to me and I couldn't catch it.

Circling two-three times around me, finally, fish entered the float; the moment it entered Father lifted the float. This time he didn't want to commit any mistake. Fish struggled to escape but it was trapped in the bundles of twigs; flapping the tail, it wrestled with Father almost for a minute.

I ran over it and cupped it up. It was the length of my hand, glossy, slippery . . .

I held that fish proudly as if I had caught it and screamed "Wooooooo . . ." a loud shriek echoed in the valley.

A big grin appeared on Father's face. The experience was most diverse and exciting one.

The voice of the fish echoed in the cave "I am a fish; once I lived happily in the depth of the river."

The first fish was in his hand and we were all hungry.

God had sent a savage gift, as an appreciative token for spending so much time in the darkness of nature.

We hadn't eaten fish before this but we couldn't give a second thought. We needed something else . . . we had been having algae for a long time. Algae was not a complete food. My taste buds had almost forgotten the taste of any other food.

I think during that time span we were looking to have something else which would improve our mental and physical strength. I was psychologically prepared to eat anything, whatever the food was and whenever it was served.

The fish was still alive and trembling; it was still gasping for air. Its cloudy eyes had popped out. We didn't want to witness the pain it was suffering through.

"Are you going to eat a living being?" my mind reared. I knocked out the doubt.

Father took no time in spearing it with a stick, not peeling the bark all the way back but just working with the pointed end. When the spearing was done, although crude, he jammed a wedge between two parts of the fish to spread it apart.

Something that looked like dark, bloody vein was running along the backbone inside. Father poked inside with a sharp stick; there was 'stuff' hanging from stringy things inside, he tried to remove as much of that messy stuff as possible.

Father then rinsed the fish with fresh river water until it was cleaned to his satisfaction.

Chime watched Father's every move grimly; a ghastly whiteness spread over Chime's face. She had never seen Father killing anyone.

Almost for an hour he prepared the fire and cleaned the fish. He pinned the fish neatly and carried it to the fire. He asked me to pick the longest stick; I picked one about my height from the bundles of sticks lying in the cave.

Father fuelled the fire until we could see red embers crackling.

He then inserted the pointed stick on either side of the backbone, making sure the fish is stable on the stick. Holding the stick over the fire he started roasting, flipping it evenly.

My eyes became attentive.

In moments, the fish was hissing and cooking with the heat; and when Father could stand the outlandish smell of fish no longer, he poked stick in along its backbone and pulled up on the flesh to check whether it's cooked.

Father took it off the fire; the once young slippery, slimy, silver fish was now wrinkled, pale grey.

We didn't want to think about its anatomy or any kind of sympathy, as it was not practical at that time.

We didn't wait for it to cool down; it had really tried our patience. My hunger piqued for the deluge to come.

This was my first time where I had such an acrimonious experience; a very uncanny feeling with highest repulsion.

Father peeled its steaming meat from under the loosened skin with his hand. I wondered how to eat; I looked at Father in disguise. Finally we decided to eat around the bones; it was opaque and flaky.

Chime tried to subtract herself from the moment. She was in a dilemma.

She said fitfully, "Brother, I can't eat this. Look, its eyes are still open and it's staring at me. I hate it." She broke out into a horrible reaction.

Picking one small portion I said, "See Chime, it's dead. We are eating it and it didn't move."

She touched the fish nervously and immediately withdrew herself. It was just beyond her comprehension. She watched us peel and eat the fish; it was a little trickier for her.

She pinched it, put the small portion in mouth, chewed and swallowed making ugly faces.

I do recall Chime feeling better while eating fish, as much as she hated to admit it.

It was a fish-fest in the cave.

We ate it. Yes, we all had it and we had it all. It had a very distinct taste but we were in no state of mind to think about it anymore.

The fish did not fill our stomachs, did not even come close. Fish meat was too light for that. But this was a good change and was also giving us the strength and courage to keep moving forwards.

After dinner, it was time to sleep and gather some strength for the next day.

Next day, at dawn we added two vital necessities to our daily routine: fishing and cooking. These activities occupied a great deal of Father's time.

There were many first times for many things, many experiences for us.

Through my clouded memory, what I do recall is one big change in the taste. In the dreadful situation of ours, fish that day turned into a feast for us.

That first time was no more first, after that there were many.

Summers allowed water bodies to exist with the rising temperature of water. Eventually, Father discovered the most likely spot from where our food would be flowing.

During those good days he was able to find and catch various water organisms using my trap bag; it was now only a question of choosing between them.

We were all changed to 'flesh eaters' but it was not by choice, it was by the necessity and demand of nature to be 'alive'. None of us were hesitant anymore in eating any sort of cooked aquatic.

That was a big change in all of us. We had completely entered and lived the Paleolithic era.

The routines imprinted in my memory include our friends, which were: 'FIRE' . . . 'TREE OF LIFE' . . . 'FOOD'.

Also now: water organisms, Chime's self created fantasy world, shadow games, books and Chime's studies; nevertheless she could not calculate the number of days we had deducted so far, but she was drawing some nice leaves on our Tree daily.

The biology of algae, our skeletal bodies and Father's food hunting at the river, his caveman outfit resembling an ape . . . an ancient man whose appearance can't be found in this era, Prayers at dusk and many more. But I don't know if I can place them in an order for you. My memories jumble from those months.

I sometimes thought, were we killing the time during those months? Or time was killing us?

Those four months were the fastest and easiest span of time, many major internal and external changes occurred in that short period of time.

How well we learned the essentials of managing energy and using our mind to conscious creations.

Reality was soon determined . . . Father's fishing weapon, 'my bag' couldn't sustain against the pressure of water anymore; it torn badly. Father tried to repair it with some grass and wooden spikes but how long could this last in front of running pressure of water?

So finally, no fish and no hunting, we were back to algae soup, and that also didn't last for more than two weeks I guess. Summer ate it all.

We all had travelled a long journey thus far but without food we were back to our tenth day in the cave when we were in a similar position suffering through hunger.

23

PRAYER

Leaf 180.

Chime felt bad for her tiny friends that we had eaten all their food. She never missed her schedule waking up, meeting and talking to her friends, although she could not serve food to them any more and was sorry for that. But her friends continued visiting the same place, daily on time, meeting Chime and of course listening to her silly talk.

After the hot salt less and tasteless soup, the only source of energy ran out, for a few days we survived on boiled water, thinking it was the same soup with missing algae.

But this was a big difference, which led us into deteriorated strength, unfilled stomachs, mania, emptiness and faintness.

Father was very weak, withered and depressed during our ongoing miserable days.

Still, many challenges were left to test our courage and willingness.

Suffering through unbearable distress we had travelled a long way. We had entered a dark tunnel; a tunnel without a single ray of light. Misery hovered over us; it was a harsh fact.

Survival was the only pleasure.

I thought, "If God made everything on earth, he is the one who guides and governs. The Power that creates all things must certainly have the power to guide and direct them. If so, nothing can happen in his great circuit of work without his knowledge or appointment and, if nothing happens without his knowledge and permission he should be aware of our dreadful condition.

If nothing happens without his consent then was he the One who had incarnated the frightful fate?"

Confused, my subconscious denied any conclusion. If God appointed all these circumstances occur to us, why did the Supreme Power do this to us? What wrong we did? Why did he save us then?

A reel of questions ran through my mind.

The answer I can think of to all these contradictions is . . .

'Life in the cave was like the annual school exam and the toughest question we had to solve was Survival.

Our Creator had put us through the exam. If we could successfully pass the final exam then He would be proud of us. Small or big, external or internal forces, every bit of this universe would be proud of our survival.'

Our existence would mean a great triumph to many universal powers but what was descending us? What external forces didn't want us to complete the journey? Were those devil powers stronger than the good spirits helping us?

We prayed to the Almighty, to our Tree of Life.
"Why are we holding on to suffering?
My conscious is ceasing.
My body, too, is badly damaged.
All my limbs are in pain.
I am coming to see my death.
What I see is a wilderness.
Here, no living beings are seen.
With no protector, I feel suffering.

We have not experienced the Happiness of the 'Deva' world—a world above human or the Happiness of the Human World either. And we will not abide in the abode of 'Nirvana'—where we can achieve the state of bliss, where all our karmic debts will be settled; either if we suffer in this Cavernous World.

What is our path? Who will be our support? There is no friend to defend us.

Who will be our protector? Since we are suffering, by which Super Natural Power shall I go?

Lord, please be our help and guide us with the ray of light to be alive, give us strength for we are in great distress."

By now, our Tree was healthy with hundreds of leaves smiling at us.

The courage, vitality and toughness our little Zanskari girl, my dearest . . . dearest . . . dearest Chime had shown against these brutal forces so far, was admirable, commendable. Though she had not been able to reach school, she had passed all the tests of life with grade 'A'.

24

DEAD AIR

Leaf 200.
Twenty days later we had traversed two hundred days of our journey.

'The Tree of Life' was getting healthier with passing time, whereas, on the contrary, we were getting thinner and gradually loosing our health.

We had long days and uneasy nights in the cave. Nature had stolen back its once worn luscious green costume. Like us, the cave was hungry too; hungry for life . . . hungry for liveliness that was missing. Dead air was looming around. Mother Earth had turned her back on the cave; she had gone unnoticed.

Being the victims of starvation lead towards our fatality; we were also the victims of certain symptoms including impulsiveness, irritability, hyperactivity, loss of body weight, decreased muscle power and endurance. Atrophy of the stomach weakened the perception of hunger due to our empty stomachs. We were too weak to sense thirst and therefore became dehydrated.

All sorts of movements were painful due to muscle atrophy and dry, cracked skin that was caused by severe dehydration.

The energy deficiency caused fatigue and rendered us more apathetic over time. I was too weak to move or even talk, my interaction with the surrounding world diminished.

There was no possible way to subsist in such an agitated state. We could not see any hope of preserving life in the absence of food intake. The impact was so violent that my weakness made me lay in bed all day.

A leisurely view of a miserable death harrowed me. My spirits sank under the burden of nature's substance, and our mental status was exhausted with the violence of starvation.

My conscious had slept so long seeing no chance to awake.

I had no divine knowledge that could be memorized.

What I had received by the good instructions of my Father, my school or monks, every bit of thinking was exhausted by an uninterrupted series of our daily physical deterioration.

We all were the most hardened, unthinking, wicked creatures existing on a thin thread of life. We lived with half of our weight.

Father and I didn't have answers to any of Chime's questions about getting food.

This ostracism reduced us all to silence . . . eventually.

The horror of dying in such a bad condition raised vapors into my head with mere apprehension.

Various scenarios filtered through my mind; something heart threatening: all three of us succumbed to death. After *Chadar* froze again, villagers would discover our bodies and mother would cry beside our bodies.

No one reading this account will expect that I am able to describe the horrors of my soul about this terrible vision. I mean, I dreamt such horrors, even while it was a dream. Nor is it any more possible to describe the impression that remained in my mind when I awoke and learnt it was but a dream. My mind was actually swaying between dream and reality.

I don't know what it was.

We lived in a terrible situation. I wanted to defeat it, but the harder I tried the more I descended into it.

The weakness and fragility of one's physical body contribute to life's uncertainty.

I find it difficult to recount those frightful days in detail, nor even coherently, for the simple reason that I can only recall it in an episodic sort of fashion.

I am still hazy about what actually happened, I was too weak to think, not in my conscious.

Hunger grasped me tightly. Through my clouded memory, what I recall were some demented recollections of the ensuing moments of that journey.

We were losing grip on reality once again.

25

WHEELS OF SAMSARA

Sometimes it is extremely difficult to maintain balance when our problems overwhelm; when dark, death and evil are part of life.

It was such a day when wickedness robed Father's mind; an idea I could never think of.

He was sitting next to my bed. Peculiar stillness was in the air; so thin the air was that we could hear our own breath. Not a leaf stirred, nor wind breathed. It looked like the calm before the storm.

Father said gloomily, "Son, we need to move on and cross this cloudy tunnel. We won't give up; there is life ahead of this."

He gathered his thoughts and continued, "What I am going to say now is logical . . . if I can think anything this moment that would save us from starving . . ." He stopped and glanced at Chime.

Breathing heavily he said ". . . is these tiny creatures."

I laid my head on his lap. This bewildering thought of his was scary and horrifying. A fearful shriek followed the silence . . .

I didn't dare to look at Chime. "Tiny creatures . . . Did Father just say that?" questioned my mind.

My mouth was dry; I was feeling too dehydrated to speak, I lay down in the stillness.

"How will she react? They are her loyal friends. This is her world; a world that distracted her from pain, hunger and mental trauma. She created this 'Chime Land'; now Father wants to destroy it so we can return our homeland safely, one day. How ruthless this act is! Should I call it an opportunity to survive?" devastated my mind asked.

I turned my head to look at Chime; she was sitting in her own alcove staring at her companions.

"Why I am elder to Chime? Why I have to taste the bitterness first, just because I am older? Father thinks I can understand the situation well. I am not old enough to understand this frightening thought of his." I pondered.

I was not strong enough to reply.

The dead air continued for some more time.

Breaking the silence he said, "Your mother will be waiting for us. We need to do this otherwise hunger will keep on driving us to the dark world. I want all of us to be safe and together as long as we can. I know you both are emotionally attached to those little beings but we all are more bound with each other. None of us can sense life ahead if something goes wrong . . ."

Stifling tears, Father moved to the other corner. My senses froze.

All I could see was darkness everywhere; I wanted to come out of it, my eyes were desperate to see the light.

My mind snagged on the idea of seeing mother. Seeing Father in tears made me follow him like a disciple.

Later, half of the day, I sprawled across my bed towards the river; Father had sat on the edge.

I experienced the most agonizing and crippling cramps ever.

I drank some water to beat the dehydration. Unaware of the reason, I drank gallons of water but still my thirst didn't quench. My stomach was fully dilated with the aquatic fluid but still the dryness of thirst was there, inside me. I sprinkled some water on my face and sat beside him.

With a dry throat, I spoke with difficulty, "What about Chime, Father? She will never allow you to do kill them and if you succeed in getting some of them onto our plates, then there is no possibility of her having them."

He said, "I know she will not allow me to do this, she will shatter. I don't want her to see it and I don't want to do it forcibly. You need to distract Chime from her corner, take her to the edge of the river and close her eyes as if you are playing blindfold."

My brain muscles lack the potency to think about it. I couldn't wait to add any mass to us. Undeniably, I obeyed.

This profound action could help slow down the grinding wheels of 'Samsara'—states of existence we pass through, bringing to a halt the cycle of suffering.

Evening settled; I moved to Chime with the impaired brain. I was disoriented and delirious.

Her emaciated body was there in the corner; looking fixedly at the caravan of visitors. Seeing her sitting there unresponsive made me realize that silence has a sound.

To draw her attention I uttered, "Chime, aren't you hungry?"

I knew somewhere that I am going to cheat her in this game.

She replied, "Did Father manage to find food? Has he got something from the river?"

I said, "Yes, you need to come with me. Father will give us something to eat today."

"Something . . . How easy it is to say something. But how will I tell her they are not something but your friends?" my heart cried out.

With our skeletal figures we moved over to Father. Chime asked, "Father, Kaba is saying you have food for us. What is it? I am hungry."

Father reverted, "Yes, do as Kaba says. I have instructed him, so if you follow and be calm and patient we will eat."

'We are going to eat'; this fact was enough for me to lie to Chime. My brain stopped thinking about evil deed . . . .

He looked at me, his deepen eyes were asking me to proceed and like a mechanical device but consciously, I obeyed him.

Reaching my bag, I picked up my school tie; who knew I would use this tie one day to deceive Chime.

"Sit facing the river, Chime." I commanded.

"But why, brother? Why I have to sit like this? Which game are we playing?" She inquired.

I said wrapping the ties around her eyes, "I am following Father's direction. He said we would get food today, trust him and be tolerant for a while."

I tightened the tie around her eyes so she would not witness the death of her friends. I sat by her side on the rock facing the might river; my hand on her shoulder.

"We wouldn't have killed Chime's friends if you would have shown us our path . . . Why did you melt untimely? How can you be so cruel?" My divested mind asked the ferociously flowing river.

I turned my head to see if Father had finished his work; he was still killing her friends. He had placed the cloth on them and was pressing them silently.

They might have screamed; they might have suffocated; we couldn't hear them, that didn't mean they felt no pain.

Something broke within me.

Seeing some living being killed and to eat it was a disgust.

Chime asked me restlessly, "What Father is doing? How long will he take to get food?" I kept quiet.

Father continued with his work. These creatures were in abundance and could give us a lot of energy. He killed many ants, earthworms, beetles, snails; all living creatures in the cave.

How would they taste? Muddy . . . soggy . . . pungent . . . ? I couldn't imagine; my brain was exhausted.

We backstabbed Chime; we killed her friends to whom she had been talking for many months. They visited her every day though we had stopped feeding them algae.

Father then splashed water on the rock; he cleaned the place where he had squashed all the insects.

"Cleaning the place with water would not wash off our sins" my inner voice warned me.

Almost half an hour passed by; killing me with each moment.

Finally, Father finished killing them; he collected all.

"Reveal Chime's eyes, Kaba. We soon will be having our food," he said.

Yellow, misty comfort faded into eternal darkness.

The smell of things, both living and dead mixed in the air. I could see hundreds of stars reflecting in the river like hundreds of candles lit by the supreme power depicting the hundreds of lives Father had nailed that day.

At last I untied the knot from Chime's eyes.

Smudging her eyes she asked, "Father, what is happening?"

She observed water dripping from the rock where her friends were living. "Why this place is wet?"

A haze of fear surrounded me. For a moment I thought what a foul luck brought us here.

Chime sensed something bad had happened there. She stepped further to meet her friends but Father held her arm and said, "The place was dirty Chime, so I washed it. Now you both help me light the fire so I can serve the food."

This time he managed to tackle the situation but I wondered how long we could act like this.

We assembled grass and wooden twigs; a while later he succeeded lighting the fire.

The dimness of light annoyed me, and the miserable reception of the death of Chime's friends; and the gloomy cave!

"What are you cooking Father?" Chime asked curiously.

Fire was bursting. To distort her thoughts Father asked Chime, "Dear, have you added the leaf today to our tree?"

She replied, "No."

"Kaba, help Chime to add leaf to our tree. Today's leaf is important. We have managed to source our food," Father said.

I nodded; wearily, balancing ourselves we both moved towards the Tree.

Father very carefully put the insects in the container; boiled the smaller ones in there and roasted the bigger ones by placing them on the hot stones, which were already red with the heat.

Suffocating darkness saturated in the cave; Father extinguished the fire as the food came to dish.

After cleaning the roasted worms, snails and other bigger ones from the fire he served them on the plate; and boiled one in soup form.

Father called us, "Kaba, Chime, food is ready, come and eat."

He said, "It's just a small quantity but good enough to feed our void stomach. No question while eating, all I can say is this will give us energy to move on. You can start."

Chime looked at her plate.

"Has she recognized them?" A daunting question ran through my mind.

To feed my dying brain I had those minuscule organisms; seeing me eating them Chime gained confidence and she started eating.

But the food was only for one night; what about the next? For how long could we hide the fact from Chime? Doing that dramatic art daily would not be possible.

Next morning, I woke up hearing mourning. Chime was weeping; Father knew the reason behind her tearful eyes. She was too young to understand what happened the other night. I moved towards her.

Bursting into tears she said, "Someone killed my friends." Speechless I sat beside her. Chime had noticed the marks of her friends where they got squeezed.

Father didn't even come near. I don't know what was going on in his mind. Was he feeling guilty?

For half a day she dissolved into tears. Her eyes were puffy and red after all the crying.

Wilderness embraced the cave.

Actuality soon stood before us. The only fact, which I understood an hour later that day, was 'hunger sees no emotions'. Father raised his voice first time at Chime.

"I killed them and we all ate them yesterday. If I hadn't killed them then we all would have died shortly. We have survived here and our destination is not away. In a few months snow will fall and we all will go back home, Chime.

She didn't respond.

At this stage going through such a brutal survival, I don't want to lose anyone of you. I can't see anyone of you dying in front of me. Will you be alright if this haunting cave being left behind with only your friends till eternity and one after one each of us die with hunger? Do you want to choose those insects over each of our lives? Will you be happy loosing any of us?"

Continuing he added, "It was the necessity to do this and I will do this daily to pass maximum of the time and safely get out from here."

Her heart was wrenched. With tearful eyes she shouted at me and Father, "You killed my friends . . . you killed my friends."

Like the cold breath of a grave, her words seemed to cut my very soul.

She was dehydrated, and sore. Sobs raked her body.

That day was just the start. After that day Father killed many parasites: bats, ants, bugs, snails and termites, all possible organisms that had life in any corner of the cave that we could roast and have. In front of Chime Father killed the tiny organism and had a small diet of them; whatever possible.

It was difficult to control Chime everyday when Father killed her little friends. With tears in her eyes after many rejections, getting scared of Father she used to sit with us and eat. She was guilty about having them.

We were surviving on insects. One by one, Father killed each of Chime's favorite colorful group of insects, small or big . . . all.

Father was not aware that at such a small place Chime was a friend with so many organisms.

I Knew Chime would always hate us for this. She even stopped talking to both of us. Though we all had got a plate of miniscule diet but it was a deadly atmosphere without Chime's voice inside the cave.

Father and I tried to get her back to life by entertaining her; we both wanted our lively Chime back who always used to have a smile on her face.

Father tried with all sorts of poor jokes, he even asked me a curious question with a joke which was left in Chime's mind: "Kaba what you guys used to do when you had to bunk arrogant Mr. Charak's class?" He asked me this question many times.

"We laugh heartily at everything professor says." I answered faking a laugh; we expected Chime to react and join us but she didn't. She was no more interested in that poor joke. She never laughed.

Sometimes, Father and I played with shadow expecting chime to join us in our game. She never ever responded to anything we did.

It is impossible for most of us to free ourselves from this web; we can only strive to be mindful of entanglement into it.

One way to do so is to reflect on how the suffering and death of sentiment can contribute to our comfort.

The manifestation of the impermanence of life and death is not a one-time event but occurs at every moment of life.

26

SPARKLING DIAMONDS

Leaf 221:
Mother Nature surprised us with her magical performance when we all had lost hope. It was a day never to be forgotten; a day that ended with miracles.

The clouds stood dark and brooding for most of the afternoon; the air was still and full of foreboding. The trees left their branches starkly silhouetted against the slate grey sky.

Chime sat at the edge of the cave by the riverside, looking closely at the world. She should have been crying, but she was too numb to even think about crying.

Father was engrossed in hunting and collecting insects in the cave, and I was busy accumulating dry grass and wooden spikes.

Swirling clouds engulfed the sky. The wind increased in intensity. I could see the trees bent precariously to one side as though they were going to fall over or get blown away like feathers.

Then, silently little ice flakes started falling in great numbers; Chime witnessed the traces of snow.

She extended her small hand out of the cave to feel its presence, to feel more snow flakes; she enveloped her wish in hands; our wish was fulfilled. We all had waited for this moment for long two hundred and twenty days; it was overwhelming when it actually happened.

Yes, it snowed.

For the very first time in so many days we heard her melodious voice.

She called, "Father . . . brother . . ." Happiness poured through her voice; her joyous face relieved our pain.

We rushed to her. Showing her hand she said, "Snow." Smile resonated on her cracked lips.

God showered his blessings upon us in the form of this white fluffy, chilling powder.

The tiny, sparkling diamonds nested on Chime's hand; she cupped as many as she could. Her hands were now filled with treasure.

This treasure could lead us back to our lost life . . . to our homeland.

A world of silver and white harmoniously mixed together. Until this time, I thought, "This is not happening to me. This is just an imagination. It can't be real!"

I scooped some snow from the ground into my hands to feel it; to feel the reality that was coming down fast at an angle in front of me.

The snow changed into silver drops, my hands trembled; I wondered whether it was cold that ran through my body, my mind or sheer happiness.

We looked at the sky, noticing the snowflakes greeting one another as they chased down towards us. Big flakes fluttered through the air obscuring our view through the shadow valley.

I watched the sky for longer . . . I concentrated into staring at grey clouds . . . the clouds swirled into some image mysteriously . . . I pierced at the image . . . swirls of the clouds formed a horse; a horse that was riding at wind's speed. A wind horse; He must have carried Maa's prayers along with him. With its uplifted energy he carried good fortune for us. Within a moment the image of the wind horse dissolved in the grey sky.

I realized soon our fateful journey would end.

The moment was winning and indescribable. We were in the realm of heaven. Silver threads of tears fell like snowy flakes.

What can I say? We were reborn.

The snow experience that day had been an immense delight for us.

Father embraced both of us.

The happiness radiated from Chime's face.

She hurried to the corner where some of her friends were dead, squeezed; some were still present in the queue, waiting for the answer for brutality from Chime.

She said, "Sorry, for whatever happened. But it's snowing outside. Now, my Father will not kill you. You all are safe!"

She looked back at us and asked Father, "Now you won't kill my friends, right, Father?" He nodded.

"Never."

Chime replied, "Promise?"

Father assured, "Promise."

Chime said, "If you kill them again I will never talk to you."

Chime hugged Father. We all sat at the edge of the cave feeling the tingle of snowflakes.

Though just a few minutes had passed, Father kept checking the river several times by dipping his hand inside to feel the icy path.

27

SECRET OF NATURE

In the village, Maa was living spiritless life; her future was locked in. But she was determined to spend the miserable remnant of her life with our Rinzin, Pema, Tashi and Diki.

An unseasonal, foggy day had gleam the sun down. She was grazing our yaks in the barren, quiet grasslands among the valleys.

The yaks were in a playful, notorious mood, and more than grazing they were jumping around enjoying the cloudy atmosphere.

Rinzin and Tashi were leaping up and down.

Other Shepherds were there too, with their cattle; unsure of weather they hauled their cattle, trying to escort them back home to save them from lightening or bad weather.

Swirling clouds surrounded the nature; with quivering hands, agitated nature dropped white grainy snow into the midst of the fog.

A funnel of snow had started high in the valley hitting the meadow at the bottom. The air in the valley was quiet and clear, the birds still circling.

Maa's diminished hope reborn. All her pain, suffering and mental anguish faded.

Her consciousness evolved around the reality.

In the fields of daydreams, she was in a dilemma. Snowflakes bestowed upon her; motionless, she stood beneath the sky to feel each granule; her world submerged. Tears resided in her eyes; she blinked them away. Thinking of nothing, she quietly contemplated this new feeling.

Looking upwards thanking God and praying for our safety, she paid gratitude.

Yaks were wandering in all different directions. Unmanageable I don't know how she controlled those crazy beings that day. She yanked them all the way down to uncle Yeshe's house, which was closer to the grassland.

She knocked his door impatiently; she couldn't wait for long. Outside on the verandah, amidst the snowfall she waited for uncle Yeshe.

He invited her in.

Along with his grandson Dawa who was about my age, uncle helped Maa tie the yaks by their verandah.

The volume of snow was getting thicker with every passing second.

Thunderous atmospheric sounds overlapped human voices. They needed to raise their voices and talk loud to overcome the dominating rumble of thunder.

Uncle said, "I told you Zampa, I have seen *Chadar* changing over the years; if it can melt untimely, then it can freeze as well without any warning. I pray for

Norbu and children's safety. I wish that *Chadar* freezes soon and they will be back to the village safely."

"I need to go the border to check *Chadar*, uncle. Will you please look after my yaks a little longer?" hesitantly she asked.

"Of course you can keep them with me."

"But, Zampa . . ." uncle explained, "It will take hours of snowfall to become *Chadar* firm to really walk on it."

Dachen came out before Maa left. He overheard the conversation between Maa and uncle Yeshe.

Seeing the snowfall he spoke valiantly, "Father, why are you raising false hopes again? You stopped me that day saying *Chadar* will freeze over soon; I said it would not form this year and I was right. For now, try to be practical, please. Why are you trying to capture what is already vanished?

His haunting tone drifted over the mountain.

More than seven months have passed. *Chadar* might have taken them underneath way back. Do you still think that they are still alive?"

Uncle Yeshe couldn't stand his bitter words; his voice crackled with anger, "Dachen, if you can't help someone you should not disappoint them." A wave of futile rage swept over him.

Uncle Yeshe assured Maa, "My soul says they will surely come back."

Even Dawa said, "Kaba will definitely come back soon aunty."

Dachen held his son's hand and walked inside, he added, "Yes, they will definitely come back but in the form of spirits at Haji's house, no chance at all Zampa."

But Maa's mind was saying something else. She ignored Dachen and said, "Uncle, thank you for being so kind and supportive; I will come in a while and take my yaks."

Uncle replied, "As you wish Zampa, you can take them whenever you want; just be careful."

His last words evaporated in the air; Maa could wait for him to finish . . . she rushed.

Standing on the verandah uncle Yeshe shouted aloud, "Try not to get wet or else you will catch cold."

But mother had no patience to listen to him; she hurriedly walked, racing the snowflakes, her mind dappled with the thought of *Chadar*.

She walked and walked and walked . . . through the land of extremes . . . crossing the sand dunes, villages resided on the mountainside, monasteries that hung high on the cliff . . . chasing the freezing winds . . .

She reached the border; few villagers were already present at the border with expectations. Snowflakes continued to tumble earthward.

They all waited the whole day watching the track.

In a due course, something unpredictable happened again.

The sun was warm, the snow was settling; melting the hearts that were gravely waiting and expecting the snow to continue.

The weather turned upside down into turmoil.

However, within a few minutes, the sky swallowed the clouds with the setting sun leaving a rainbow behind reflecting sadness, sorrow, emptiness, suffering, misery, evil and death . . .

The colors of the rainbow diminished brightness of their joy.

Maa was among them. Her hopes faded further into the distance. She wanted to drink the river dry.

The water reflected the crimson sky. The last light of the day tinted the air and the earth.

She sat by the riverside with other visitors; night spread its wings. But sooner or later everyone left without hopes, without expectations. Secret of Mother Earth peered through her wounded soul.

Dimness spread in valley, night was stark, the roads were empty when she reached Uncle Yeshe's house to collect our yaks.

Uncle was waiting for her . . . seeing her at the entrance of his verandah he moved ahead. There was nothing he could say. He simply untied our yaks and handed over to my mother.

28

FORTUITOUS ENCOUNTER

The valley was silent; gravely stillness resided in the cave.

We breathed simply to see snowfall once again.

My heart cried out loud in sheer misery at the hopelessness of life . . . our life.

Once again we descended into the darkness.

Weather transformed drastically; the cloudless sky veiled our fate.

In the morning we had witnessed snowfall; a day or two more and we would be journeying back to our home . . . trailing on *Chadar* . . .

But our destiny was something else. Chilling breeze robbed snow by the evening. Each phenomenon lasted for a few hours.

To walk on the glassy track, to see Maa, our yaks and to live in our home was nothing but an agonizing dream.

We lay awake all through the night; looking outside the cave impatiently, staring at the sky with endless desire; one by one the stars winked on in a darkening sky.

That miserable night was impossible to conceive. The snowfall that day had brought hope along . . . who knew it would be tangible.

My mind assured me, "Our friend 'HOPE' would not lead us to disappointment. It is an indication . . . any moment the path would reappear. God can't be so cruel."

Lying in my bed I pleaded, "Mother Earth, please show your magic tricks once again . . . unveil the curtain of our doubts . . . send snow the way you did in the morning . . . our destiny . . . our existence is in your hands. Help us to get out of this cavernous life . . . show us path."

My mind told me, "It snowed in the morning when there was no hope, no sign . . . that means it will snow soon . . . may be mid-night . . . probably at dawn . . . or sometime tomorrow indeed."

"Winter is on its way; *Chadar* will appear soon" beamed my helpless mind.

We spent most of the time sitting at the edge of the river; waiting with hungry eyes, thirsty mind and haunted thoughts.

But we were not fortunate to witness a day with snowfall. We were left with timeless journey in this unremitting black hole.

The third day after we witnessed snowfall, it was leaf 224 . . . God offered us something else . . .

We hadn't eaten anything for three days as Father had promised Chime that he would not kill her friends anymore. He was trying to keep his words as far as he could.

The wind was dead; we had sat on the edge of the river looking into the distance. Suddenly, Father's eye caught a glimpse of something floating down river in our direction.

Fogged had draped river.

Hurriedly Father stood up, narrowing his eyes he tried to catch sight of floating thing; stuffed jute like being floated towards us slowly.

Impatiently, Father rushed into the cave; picked up the two thickest, longest wooden sticks and exited within a flash of time.

Lifeless, Chime and I were still sitting.

Struggling, we both stood up; Father's hasty activity caught our attention.

A long—legged, uncoordinated dead body floated on the freezing river; passing a few obstacles; greeting all corners of the river.

The large animal body was marching towards the cave; before it would flow away further and we would lose it, Father tied both the sticks together to catch it and stood at the edge of the river.

This was the most fortuitous encounter.

With the help of two sticks Father tried to pull that rigid body.

He instructed, "Kaba, help me drag the body." I held his right hand and I felt nothing but bones; his body had emaciated drastically; to drag the animal all by himself was tiresome.

We both started pulling it towards us with all our strength; my body muscles stretched while pulling it up, I felt a weight on my wrists and my ankles. To catch the body against the repulsive force of the water was laborious.

It bounced off the edge several times; finally Father managed to sidetrack caramel brown body. He pulled its large black hooves and grabbed one of the legs, then the second and lastly with the rest of his energy we fetched it up and dragged it inside the cave.

Lifeless, gruesome, massive body was before us. It was a dead reindeer!

It might have fallen through thin ice and drowned. Its death-like beady black eyes, devoid of all emotions were wide open; it was an awful sight.

Chime was distressed and didn't feel comfortable; she stared at the corpse with a grim and shuddering fascination.

For food we could count upon reindeer for a longer period; and it could be the only source of our survival.

God had offered alms; to reject an offering would be an offense.

A while later, Father parted a fraction of it, separated the skin; a foul, unbearable smell came out of it. But this was the only food we had captured since past few months.

We were sure that we could easily survive over this meat for the remaining days in case Chadar wouldn't form soon. It was good food and a good quantity meal for us. Father was able to keep his promise of not killing Chime's friends.

Father said, "How we are going to preserve this meat? I must remove the moisture to prevent it rotting."

But first of all we had to suppress the shouting, hungry demons inside our stomachs.

Father cut the meat into pieces; "Kaba, wash these pieces with water," Father said.

I was hesitant to touch it.

But hunger commanded my mind; I washed away the cut blood stained pieces with the chilled flowing water.

Chime stood behind me, with cold feet. She was horrified and hesitant to come any nearer to the ever-open eyes of the spiritless carcass.

I brought the clean pieces of meat inside.

Father was rubbing stones to ignite the fire. Within a short time, fire erupted. By now, with experience in our rocky shelter, he had excelled in such activities.

He skewered the pieces into the pointed end of the stick; flipping it for a considerable amount of time he roasted it. I hated the smell wafted through the roasted meat.

"If I can't even bear its smell then how I'm ever going to stand the taste?" I wondered.

The meat became firmer, dark brown outside and red inside; Father took it out of the fire to check whether it was completely cooked. Yes, it was!

Eventually, Chime remained unsure about the cooked meat; I don't know if the taste of the meat bothered her or it was her psychology about eating an animal.

We didn't wait for long. Following Father, I sliced off a chunk the size of *momo* and gasped and had the first bite; it was chewy and meaty. It took me back to the Paleolithic era.

The texture was more difficult to adjust than the taste.

It was bland and tender . . . a taste I can't really describe. The flavor was not overwhelming though; my taste buds refused to react.

Father insisted, "Chime, eat . . . you must eat this to save your insect friends. It will give you strength to walk on *Chadar*."

The idea of eating an animal was not digestible but our 'SURVIVAL' was hungry and dying.

Nothing that I loved the taste but it definitely tasted better than insects.

After fish, the best food out of the worst things we had put into our mouths. Subsequently, with shaky hands, Chime picked the slice of roasted meat without challenging her small brain.

To save her insect friends she finally had her portion of food; willingly or unwillingly didn't matter. After a long time we had a stomach filling meal. Food that could help us survive.

None of us felt bad or guilty that day; the food was not killed but delivered. Chime was happy because with this unexpected delivery her remaining friends were safe.

After eating the stomach filling meal, to preserve the rest of the meat, we skinned it up, rinse the inside thoroughly with water and cut the edible portion of it into pieces.

The waste decaying parts we threw into the flowing water. The meat was in bulk; the task was tedious mainly with no proper cutting tools. Whatever portion we cut that day, Father covered it with his thin blanket, sprinkling a lot of chilled water over.

It was a hectic day full of engaging activities.

We didn't even realize how the day ended so soon. Exhausted we fed off to sleep.

The snow didn't show up, however the nights were colder. But we had enough fuel to keep the fire going whenever required.

We continued with the same preserved carcass for a few days; despite the fact the flesh of the reindeer was decomposing and disintegrating by each hour.

29

GENTLE WHISPERS

Autumn mists drifted up the river, frost—nipping winds left their spoor in the hoar mornings killing the leaves. Cold winds chased the warmth of the day.

I drew the leaf on our Tree numbering it 234.

Early afternoon, we all had our only food . . . roasted meat.

Later, I sat with Chime to teach her new lesson; by now, she had excelled in learning A to Z alphabets.

"Chime, today I am going to teach you how to spell words," I said.

She was overjoyed to hear that. "Brother, teach me to write my name today," she exclaimed.

I nodded with approval. She picked up the last pencil from my toolbox; its extensive use had shortened its life. All my wax colors were overused; we saved few to draw a leaf everyday on our 'Tree of Life.'

"Chime, right C," I instructed.

She held a pencil in her left hand, adjusting its point she asked, "Brother 'C' for?"

I answered 'C' for 'Cave'. I could say 'C' for Cat; but for us, to relate to the cave was easier, after spending two hundred and thirty four days in this cavernous hollow.

Talking aloud Chime wrote in her notebook 'C.' Her letter 'C' looked like horizontal letter 'V.'

"Write H," I stated.

"H for Home?" she asked me.

I nodded, "Yes."

"When will we reach our home, brother?" she questioned.

"Chime, no other queries while studying," Father interrupted to avoid answering her question. She squirmed.

"Now write I." I noticed Chime's hands were shaking; her palms were moist.

She paused holding her head with hands and then started vomiting.

Father rushed towards us, "Chime, dear . . . what's wrong?"

She was not able to answer; I couldn't understand what happened to her; few minutes earlier she was all fine, talking to me, studying.

Father said, "I guess, it is the meat . . . she couldn't digest it."

I opened up her bedding and asked her to rest. Chime quietly reclined on it. An hour later Chime got up, stumbling and running towards the edge of the cave, she vomited again.

She freshened up at the edge of the cave, near our riverside daily spot. Father helped her to clean up and wash her face with fresh water.

He advised, "Sleep for a little longer, Chime."

She lay there, disoriented and shaky. Sweat started dripping down her body.

Everything was fine during the actual eating phase. She lost a lot of vital body fluids due to indigestion. Father thought a good nap would work for her.

The day was miserable. I was perplexed about what to do. If we had been in Ladakh School, we would have had some medicine from the school staff. If we were at home in Zanskar, Maa would have given Chime a hot medicine bath with some herbs to stop her vomiting. Or might be monk would have treated her with blessed pills or blessed water.

We didn't have anything in the cave. We were entirely helpless. I was tense and feeling bad about her health.

I prayed to the good spirits from the heaven to come down and rescue her from the pain she was suffering.

I sat beside her, waiting for her to wake up.

Time slowly melted away, over the course of a couple of sleepless hours, her vomit stopped and her normal health resumed.

By evening time, she got up. I asked, "How are you feeling now?"

She replied faintly, "I am better."

I didn't feel like having an evening meal.

No moon, no stars, only silence fell with the light.

Darkness seeped into every corner of the cave, every crack of the wall, stealthily. With judgment, I placed my bedding next to Chime quiet early that night.

Father rested beside us.

Lying on our respective bedding, Chime and I went on talking; we were not feeling sleepy, so our discussions went on till late.

She was thinking, reciting and giving me an account of all she had learned from me so far. Alphabets, numbers; I felt good being a teacher and testing her knowledge.

Finally, Father was troubled by our continuous babble and interrupted, saying, "Chime, Kaba, go to sleep soon. How much do you need to talk? Can't you be quiet and go to sleep?"

Then addressing Chime, he added, "Daughter, if you talk so much, you'll feel sick again. Sleep for now; talk as much you want after waking up tomorrow."

We stayed mute for a minute. Chime couldn't hold the silence for long, she exclaimed, "Father I am not feeling sleepy. I am all well and will not vomit now, I promise."

Father said, strictly, "No, go to sleep. I don't want to hear a single word from you now. Save some of your talking for tomorrow."

Later, we still continued whispering for some more time and with Chime's bird like humming, God knows when I went to sleep.

Her gentle whispers dissolved into the darkness.

30

ETERNAL SILENCE

Leaf 235.
Blood red streaks of twilight were fading;
I awoke later than usual because of our prolonged gossips the previous night. The intense brightness of the sun hit my eyes hard as I opened them.

Chime was still sleeping.

The coldness of early winters advanced. An icy sharpness was in the air.

Engaged in his daily search activities at the edge of the river, Father was soaking up the sunlight.

Chime often woke up earlier than I every morning; but that day, I did.

With the morning tide as day cracked, whenever I had opened my eyes I saw Chime talking with her friends. That day Chime was not in her place; it was an imperfect picture; her friends were waiting for her.

I didn't think of disturbing her because of the delayed late night sleep. I moved close to her friends to look at them and sat there for some time.

After a while, I went over to Chime to wake her up. I wanted to start studying. The previous night's studious talks had been good. She was a quick learner. That day onwards I decided to teach her how to read the time; but before that, she had to finish writing her name.

Calling several times I tried to wake her up, "Wake up Chime, your friends are waiting for you." I said.

I kept on calling her but she was in a deep sleep. "Chime, wake up. You have to finish writing your name ten times; you haven't even finished writing it once." I continued.

Father said, "Kaba, don't disturb her. Let her sleep for some more time. Both of you were talking till late last night. I told her several times to sleep but she never listens to me. She vomited and drained an abundance of energy yesterday and still she kept on chatting. So much she talks! Oh Lord, I wonder how much energy God has given to her to talk, this little puppet can't remain silent, it's good . . . a little silence at the moment."

Afternoon shadow dappled the ground. When still she didn't wake up, some of her friends . . . flies and ants, decided to pay a visit to see Chime on her bed.

They were humming around her. Earlier there were a few, but later there were so many, I guess every living creature inside the cave: small or big, crawling, flying came over to Chime to wake her up.

In a few minutes, there were plenty creatures around her.

Father was drying all twigs and sticks he had collected from River.

I tried to drive off the surrounding creatures away from her but they kept on impeding. I was constantly trying to wake her up but she didn't respond.

I screamed, "Father, there are many ants and flies around Chime. She is not waking up."

Father walked up to us. He bent down on his knees to see Chime; his face turned yellow, blood drained from his face. His expression changed.

Trying to ward off the flies Father yelled, "Chime, get up."

Father checked her nerve by holding her wrist, he moved his head closer to her nose to check her breath, his fingers trembled and within a matter of seconds everything changed.

I froze; my throat constricted. He didn't reply, his pitch-black eyes, impossible to read, very scary.

Something horrible had happened. He shook her violently to wake her up, but she didn't react. A chill of fear ran through me.

His eyes were staring in disbelief.

"Don't die," he quavered, in tones of lugubriousness. Painful tears seeped down his face. Holding Chime in his arms he cried inaudibly, and then let it rip; he cried as if his heart had been ripped from his body.

"Come on Chime, wake up and talk . . . Your friends are around you . . . waiting for you . . . they are hungry . . . algae is growing up . . . we both will feed them . . . please get up and talk to Kaba. I won't stop you from talking; even I will sit beside you and listen to your chatter all night . . . Please get up for once . . . please Chime, please . . ." he was begging.

"Your mother, your yaks, everyone is waiting for you, what will I tell them? Next year I will surely take you to school and buy a new uniform for you . . . and . . . and . . . and I will never kill your friends . . . I promise . . . I promise . . . but please get up my baby . . ." he pleaded.

My stomach turned into ice . . . something struck my mind.

Tears poured against my dry pale cheeks like rivulets; shock robbed me of speech. I witnessed the death of my own sister in front of me.

The cold dark night pierced my every bone.

Father kept on crying, hugging the fragile body of our angel in his hands, he hugged me and said, "Chime left us Kaba, my little baby left us all . . ." Paralyzed with fear, I didn't reply.

All my emotions rolled down in the form of silent water from my stony eyes making me benumbed.

Nature had twisted its knot.

31

YAKS

At smoky grey dawn early winter wind crept into the valley; an agitated grunting woke my Maa up. The sound was uneasy, hungry as if it was calling her; it disturbed spirits in the valley.

Distracted, Maa rushed out of the room, our yaks were hovering on the verandah; they never behaved like this before.

Rinzin and Pema wailed plaintively, Diki and Tashi were visibly distressed. They gestured with their horns; it seemed they were trying to talk to Maa.

Maa tried to feed them fodder but they refused to eat. She couldn't milk them that day; they were uncontrollable for no apparent reason.

This was the very first time she had faced this strange behavior from them; Maa did not understand the reason. She pampered them, but they didn't calm down.

Maa missed her daily routine. They were grunting for more than an hour. When Maa touched Rinzin, her heart was racing and she was shaking.

Pema lay down, flat stretched out, looking as if dead.

They stood in vigil after some time. Maa noticed water rolling down their eyes. She understood they suffered through something, but what?

She examined them to find if they were hurt or had been poisoned . . . or someone had cast black magic.

She was trying to find a reason behind their abnormal behavior, but couldn't find any.

In the afternoon, clouds gathered as if reluctant to leave; moving back and forth in the air.

They got furiously irresistible and became unmanageable for Maa; they wanted to flee. Pema stood up on her hind legs, and started licking and smelling the air with her head straight up. Rinzin sucked in a breath.

Mother got a chill in her legs.

The whole day they didn't eat; their moist eyes never dried.

The secrets were locked away.

32

SHADOW PLAY

Under a never setting sun, Father sat near Chime, haunted by lost empire. Dark night advanced, Chime's pale hand was still in his hands; our sleep deprived, hunger died, desire to live was slaughtered . . . creepy silence spread inside the cave.

No more suffering, no more hunger; peacefully, quiet Chime lay in Father's arms.

Like the cold breath of a grave, her words pierced my very soul.

Amid the dead air in my head . . . in my heart . . . echoed one, two, three, four . . . her counting, she had uttered in her sweet voice.

"C for Cave . . . H for Home . . ." the alphabets hit my mind hard.

The other day she was all excited about writing her name in the notebook; now, she was no more in this world.

She couldn't even finish writing her name; nor could she complete her journey from cave to home.

Chime was in the new realms of the unknown; sleeping soundly as if dreaming.

"This time, her dream was prolonged. Many visitors had certainly arrived to see her: Maa, Rinzin, Pema, Tashi, Diki, all her tiny friends in the cave and how could she finish her dream without visiting school?" I thought.

It was an immortal departure of a mortal coil; she was bidding a farewell to the world.

Father lay awake all through the night by her side. Later, getting up, picking up our walking sticks and spear like wood he moved to the place where Chime used to feed her friends.

Father started digging the place . . . our 'Chime Land.'

He had to be strong to endure the task of digging his own daughter's grave . . . our Chime's grave.

He always wanted to send her to the school . . . and there he was . . . sending her to her grave; to bury her was his destiny.

The soil was as hard as the situation.

Father took momentary rests while digging the grave.

"Kaba, come and help me," he uttered in a gravely voice. But I didn't move . . . not even by an inch. My spirit left my body, and I was taken to outer darkness. I began to feel the anguish and torment of that terrible place.

I was frozen in time and space . . . motionless.

Father screamed, "Chime is your sister, please help me and give your hand in granting her place to rest in peace forever."

He kept on yelling but I didn't respond.

"Her place is not here . . . not in this grave. But in the realm of Human." My mind cried out.

When Father asked me to play with her, I did. When he asked me to walk with her throughout our *Chadar* journey, I did. When he asked me to teach her, I did.

But then, he needed me to help him dig her grave . . . the truth annoyed me and the miserable reception of her decease.

I saw Father's shadow on the wall . . . his shadow was digging the grave. Chime's motionless, fragile shadow lay on the floor.

The little princess was sleeping. Father's gloomy shadow made up her bed. A few more hours and I knew she would rest on her bed forever; her shadow would no more play with me.

I asked my shadow, "Why things are not looking the same? Why Chime's shadow is missing?"

The day had lost its presence.

The distant star magnified the silence; Father was still working.

On the second night, holding Chime's hand in his, he sat his cavernous eyes looking into another world; his face frozen in a glassy stare of horror. I was fearful; how could I not be fearful of the night that was shrouding the world in front of me in pitch-black darkness?

The next morning, after two to three hours of unearthing, he managed to create a pit in the ground, deep enough to cuddle our little Chime.

Finishing his digging, he washed out his mouth.

I was still frozen . . . traumatized I had sat in the same corner for the past two days. I felt the blood cease to circulate; the tips of my toes went numb, then my feet, ankles, knees, stomach and heart. My spirit began to descend . . .

My thoughts, my soul, my body, my voice was concealed . . . scared to confess what I was feeling.

Father lifted Chime's body with his weaker hands and carried it near the river. He bathed her before her last journey to the other world. Afterwards, he came inside the cave and opened her bag to take out some other clothes for her.

Thoughtfully, he then dropped her bag and opened mine; he removed my school uniform.

The idea of wearing school uniform always fascinated Chime . . . she was eager to wear it. If we had successfully reached Ladakh School that year then her wish would have been fulfilled.

Father managed to dress her up in my uniform. This was the costume she always dreamed of wearing some day.

Father called me, "Kaba, this is your sister's last journey of this lifetime, you must give a hand to perform the final ritual."

Something pushed me; I walked up to the river for the first time in the past two days.

I moved physically following Father's instructions; my emotions ceased, mind stagnant.

There were no monks to prepare her funeral, to chant verses, to release the good energies from her fading personality. There were no alms to offer.

Here, at this funeral, her family was Father, all her tiny friends and me . . . the cave . . . the river . . . the sky and our Tree of Life.

Tree of Life had lost its life.

Chime had been adding leaves to tree for its longevity, who knew she would cheat on her own Life.

Father and I lifted Chime's body and took it to the grave.

He chanted some mantras. Going to the riverbank, he offered water as alms to Goddess Mother Earth like a monk to create goodwill for her spirit.

And the next moment she was there . . . sleeping inside the grave. She descended into another world . . . it was a never-ending nap.

Her infectious smile lit up the cave, only her voice faded.

Tears obscured my vision. Father planted a kiss on her forehead, "Pray for her, Kaba . . ." he said.

Looking upon her body the very last time I said good-bye to her.

Devastated I looked at Father's shadow; it was wrapping Chime's shadow in its dark arms giving her last place to sleep.

Death and Shadow encircled one another.

I asked my shadow to help me find Chime's shadow, which was long gone from sight.

I felt like a stranger inside the cave. I wanted to outcast my shadow. I wanted to run away from it as fast as I could to catch Chime's shadow.

I don't know which part I was playing in that shadow game but I had no courage to face her.

I turned my back to her.

I broke my promise that I would play until we wouldn't get out of the cave . . .

I walked away. Father tried to stop me but I didn't.

Menacing shadows were still creeping. We were venturing into the dark unknown world of our shadows. It was the first time I had been scared of shadows . . . ghostly shadows.

Father covered the grave with mud placing a heavy stone on top of it.

Fluttering from the autumn trees, every leaf was blessing the only flower: 'Chime'.

'Life is nothing but a false belief . . . a false appearance . . . A conception created by imagination having no objective reality, just like shadows.'

For years, we didn't go without talking, without her bubbling over with warmth and then—she was gone; hidden behind a veil of silence.

After Chime, I was now lodged in darkness for eons.

33

DISTANT STAR

Chadar could take us underneath on the snowy terrain, avalanche could swallow us; snow leopards could feed on us.

Wild nature, hungry predators could lead us to death and we would have died together; I would never have seen Chime in her grave.

Death watched upon us standing outside the cave; a single wrong step and we would be in the arms of death.

But destiny had her plans. My sister had passed away of something really stupid . . . a stomach infection.

Prior to this, she had passed all the tests of life so bravely. She had fearlessly travelled and came so far on this journey with a love for nature, insects and every creation of God.

Chime was not around, yet every atom in the air was surrounded with her thoughts, silly acts and her sugar coated voice.

After this trauma, mere my soulless body existed in the cave.

Day and night linked together followed each other.

The cave, river, valleys and trees were demonstrating and expounding the unsurpassed, ultimate truth.

The word 'Survival' lost its meaning. Life was an aimless journey with no desire for a destination.

Our senses were ceased; we filled our stomachs with algae.

Weeks passed, I didn't utter a single word.

Father was worried about me; he was dying of stress, silence, tension and frustration.

"What I am going to tell your mother? I couldn't take care of her daughter?"

"Rinzin and Pema must be waiting for her," he kept murmuring.

Father tried to perform every possible activity of Chime to get me out from that traumatic condition of mine.

Father tried to play shadow games to awaken my senses . . . to make me laugh. He attempted all possible shadows. Animals, fish, birds; they wiggled and waggled, walked, jumped, swam, ran and flew but for me they all were dead . . . deadly shadows that scared me to death, reminded me of my Chime.

Sometimes I witnessed shadows around . . . shadows of Maa, shadows of Yoko.

I woke up at nights with paranoid delusions. I failed to perceive them; in fact they existed much like '*Maya*'—the magical appearance.

All the visions that I saw in my life in the cave were like a dream—under the influence of ignorance, I believed all the objects existed apart from causes and condition. My visions were infrequent and had been happening for a long time. To count every last one to give an exact frequency will take a lifetime.

We both were present inside the cave, but I was devoid, and my spiritless presence made Father all alone . . .

Every morning Father fed Chime's friends with chunk of algae, just like Chime did after waking up.

Sometimes he recited the alphabet, nursery poems, blabbered silly things and stories in the same rhythmic manner of hers.

Depicting stupidly childish shadows on the walls, he mimicked her; this entire he did alone like a five-year-old girl.

Standing on the edge of the river he shouted like a mad person to shed his frustration.

His face was a barren landscape of sorrow, parted by rivers of tears.

Except our 'Tree of Life', our companions 'HOPE', 'STRENGTH', 'FAITH' and 'TOGETHERNESS' abandoned us.

Father nurtured the tree by adding leaves and giving them numbers. Chime always wanted to see that tree fully grown.

I inhaled and exhaled the air; but for me, this was not breathing.

Chime stole away our liveliness and souls, leaving us behind, suffering.

She was everyone's favorite. Why did God take her away? Why didn't he take us all together? My mind was so filled with Chime's thoughts that one night, I woke up.

Father had slept in his place.

With impaired judgments, crossing Father, I moved ahead in an altered state of consciousness.

I walked up to the grave; Father was unaware of my state.

Like a distant star under black-inked sky, I sat near her grave for a while, then after some time, something happened to me as if I was possessed.

I started removing the mud from the surface, the stone was still in its place; I dug around the surface.

While excavating the grave, at some point my stick struck the stone; hearing the smooth, disrupted voices Father got up.

When the voices didn't stop, in the darkness, following the sound he called me, "Kaba, Kaba, Kaba?" he swept his hand across my bedding to confirm my presence but couldn't find me there.

Shouting for me twice . . . thrice, his eyes located me in the dark near the grave, digging up mud.

Father ran towards me grumbling, "Kaba, what are you doing?" holding me, trying to control me, he said, "Your sister is sleeping there."

He tried to get my trembling body back into consciousness but I didn't feel a thing.

Picking me up, he carried me to bed; that night holding my hand in his, he lay beside me until the next morning. His mouth set in a hard, grim line . . . his eyes speculative.

34

BLACK WORLD

*A*fter that night, day by day, my mental and physical health continued diminishing.

The space was filled with emptiness; there was no sign of sleep, hunger, sound or desire. Only my tears depicted intricate part of my soul.

The cave ached in wild solitude.

Once savior cave turned into a demon that swallowed our Chime.

It became a haunted place for me. I was spending my time in an entirely black world . . . lurking in the shadows. I was descending into the darkness until the lights of the earth faded; it was an awful feeling. I tried to claw my way back up but failed.

Father tried hard to drag me back into the real world. My thoughts were paralyzed.

My unconscious state prolonged uncertainly; Father could not predict how long I would be in an elusive state . . . for days, weeks, months or indefinitely? He was trying in vain to communicate with me, trying to bring immense reassurance.

Nothing was working for me. He had already lost his heart with dearest Chime, and he could not afford to lose me.

At times he yelled at me . . . slapped me . . . begged me; he was as strict as a teacher, as kind as a mother and as friendly as a sister . . . he played all the roles he could. He never succeeded in stopping my tears.

I can only recall his blur face flashing in front of my eyes, trying to show me our 'Tree of Life.'

I only remember his tremulously quivering words, "Kaba, only a few days are left . . . we will go back, please . . . please . . . do not give up. I won't be able to live. I won't be able to return to Zanskar with this burden. I am too weak and old . . . please be with me. Do not leave your Father alone this way."

His every word drifted away.

Chime's death had grieved me greatly.

The spirits were testing the limits of human endurance.

In the dithering cold night, shivering with chillness trying to close my eyes, I saw the blurred outline of my Father's lean, hazed figure drawing leaf number 265.

35

THE WINDY NIGHT

Leaf 265.

The night was Chilly and windy. I was extremely weak; the cold had numbed my brain.

Father was trying to light the fire. The cool and soft breeze turned into a strong gale. Stormy clouds hovered in the sky; wind blew restlessly, vigorously.

He couldn't generate the heat to create fire because of mighty climate and moisture in the air.

The moist air loomed over the mountains; temperature went on decreasing with traces of snow falling outside. Father ignored the snowfall because of its uncertainty. His only priority was my health.

To rely on any absurd certainty and to think that *Chadar* would freeze earlier than it's time was senseless. There was no room for possibilities and uncertainties.

A few days ago the traces had spoiled our happiness . . .

We were bullied by nature . . .

That time, due to prior experience Father expected the snowfall for a few hours only, and he was certain it would melt before next morning.

There was still one complete branch left, waiting for its leaves to be drawn.

My teeth were chattering, my organs started responding slowly.

Seeing my shivering body, he covered me with all possible clothes and blankets available inside.

My muscles twitched, sitting beside me for hours he was rubbing my palm and soles.

All night he didn't rest for a single minute.

The wild troubling violent breezes continued for the entire night. Tension hovered as thick as fog.

Father didn't leave the hold of mine for even a second. He was afraid that the coldness of roaring wind would swipe me away from him and I would leave him any moment like Chime.

36

FRIENDS FOREVER

Leaf 266.
The Skies had dawned with a clear, blazing blue. Father was by my side holding my hand.

He was calling me, "Kaba, Kaba . . ."

Under such a miserable supposition, when time had disclosed all, I woke up with heavy eyes.

Father asked, "Are you alright, Kaba?"

I was looking into some other world; the realms of hell . . . the worst place where one finds the most suffering.

He was relieved to see me regaining my ability to move.

Leaving my hand, he went outside to freshen up.

The cold wind was still lingering, leaving the atmosphere foggy.

He dipped his hand into the river to splash water on his face, and it hit a hard, thick layer; he didn't believe what he had felt.

After many days, the very first time, he felt the toughness of the layer.

Tranquil grey clouds had made the atmosphere hazy, leaving vision unclear.

Before his frozen mind could think of anything, a single shaft of autumn sunlight cutting through the fog fell on his palm, clearing the visuals of land.

The bright rays captured the earth; overtaking the smoky surroundings.

It was a deep current of change; a heart stopping moment for him.

Should Father be happy, seeing frozen *Chadar*? Were our weak, thin bodies capable enough to cross the icy, dangerous path? Should he be happy for taking me home alive from there? But Was I alive?

We were safe and would be going back to Zanskar. But what would he tell mother when she would ask about Chime? What would he say to yaks? How would he face them and explain devastating Facts?

He came inside and drew the leaf number 266 on the eighth branch on our 'Tree of Life'.

With eight branches, the Tree grew stronger.

Its first branch spoke of 'Luck'. When Father cheated on death despite of getting trapped underneath *Chadar*; it was our luck. When snow leopards didn't feed on us; yes, it was our luck.

I enjoyed the brotherhood most when in the cavernous home I taught Chime how to write numbers and alphabets; it's second branched showered 'Joy' upon us under such miserable conditions.

Its third branch invoked Father's 'Brilliance' and he invented fire.

The fourth branch magically turned spring into summer; rains engulfed summer and asked us not to lose 'Hope.' It assured us that few more months, one day it would snow and we all would return home.

In the mysterious domain, the fifth branch tasted our 'Patience', we all struggled to be patient; and as a result it gifted us fish.

In the sixth month when I had succumbed to reality, when hunger had gripped our being, the sixth branch served us insects and bestowed us with 'Endurance.'

When the seventh branch offered us reindeer we achieved 'Sustainment.'

True, the eighth branch of our Tree of Life blessed us with 'Longevity' by providing us food and fire; by teaching us to be patient and have faith in the Supreme Power. It gave us Life, but in return snatched our Chime as an offering.

Picking me up in his arms, Father moved to Chime's grave.

We both sat for a long in front of the grave. He didn't want to leave our little Chime there alone.

The next thing he saw gave him courage to proceed . . . with a heavy heart.

A few ants and other insects were coming out of Chime's grave, small colorful flying creatures had joined them and all together they formed Chime's Smiling face.

THEY WERE HER TRUE PARTNERS AND FRIENDS WHO WILL ALWAYS BE WITH HER, TAKING CARE OF HER 'FOREVER'.

One by one Father collected all her belongings: sleeping bag, her clothes, Tiffin; our notebooks and pencil box that were lying in one corner. He picked up the notebook and flipped through it.

Father examined her handwriting for a long time. Like her handwriting her life, too, was crooked; Father read aloud "C . . . H . . ." the only letters she could manage to write. Destiny didn't even allow her to finish writing her name in the notebook.

Father opened my pencil box only to find it filled with pencil shavings; Chime had collected and saved them all.

Father scooped all her saved pencil shavings from my pencil box and offered them to her grave.

A cold, crisp wind carried them away. They started swaying as if some divine intervention, as if they were ready to travel with Chime . . . further away into the distance.

Father picked up luggage, Chime's bag and hoisted me onto his shoulder. Looking back he glanced at our 'Tree of Life', its every branch and at leaves Chime once made on it.

The 'Tree of Life' was our only companion whom we abandoned.

Father lifted his first foot forward after two hundred and sixty six days . . . almost eight months after.

He took a few more steps, checking the firmness of trail with walking stick; he moved ahead balancing himself on the icy path. After walking a few feet away from the cave, he turned, looking back at the lifeless void where he was leaving his heart behind; she didn't notice us.

We ventured into empty abode . . . . On the verge of losing our footing on slippery ground, we continued our trek home.

The valley was filled with an eerie silence. The hollow sound of footsteps was echoing, crunching the snow under the feet. Sky was bruised; the paradise was lost; the color palette washed off, leaving greys behind.

The nightmare that confronted us will always be etched in my mind.

37

CHIME

Months Later.

One night, I was lying on my bed near Father with my eyes open; Maa too, lay on her bed restlessly.

The mask, I had got from the monastery to scare Chime was hung on the wall; I stared at it. Who knew that Chime, once scared of that mask, would deal with her own life so bravely?

I felt as if wearing that mask she was scaring me away, teasing me that she had won. She had finally managed to scare me to death.

Father heard the same lines Chime had uttered in the cave, the same poetry, Chime used to rhyme in the cave. Father immediately got up from his bed and moved outside; Maa followed him.

They saw a girl almost of the same age as Chime walking down the lane, singing to her father; same poetry Chime used to sing in the cave.

That girl resembled our little Chime.

They felt her presence immensely.

The soothing sound leaving its spellbinding effects lingered on my mind likes a 'Wind chime'.

Father fell on his knees; clutching his head in despair. Tears streamed down my cheeks; tears that I thought had dried up from the grief of Chime's death.

I kept my voice inside, locked away from myself. The pain didn't replace other feelings but only hide them from sight.

Only the wheel of life was spinning.

All I could remember was Chime talking to me that night, in her voice the numbers and alphabets.

Father and Maa took me to Haaji's place, to monasteries . . . wherever possible to cure. Monks treated me with blessed water, blessed pills that contained the relics of previous great meditators; but nothing worked for a long time. It took years for me to come out of trauma . . .

Her 'chimmy' face is still present around me . . .

She will always be everlasting like her name 'CHIME.'